MISRECOGNITION

MADISON NEWBOUND

SIMON & SCHUSTER

New York   London   Toronto   Sydney   New Delhi

100
YEARS
SIMON &
SCHUSTER

1230 Avenue of the Americas
New York, NY 10020

First Simon & Schuster hardcover edition July 2024

SIMON & SCHUSTER and colophon are registered trademarks of Simon & Schuster, LLC

Simon & Schuster: Celebrating 100 Years of Publishing in 2024

For information about special discounts for bulk purchases, please contact Simon & Schuster Special Sales at 1-866-506-1949 or business@simonandschuster.com.

The Simon & Schuster Speakers Bureau can bring authors to your live event. For more information or to book an event, contact the Simon & Schuster Speakers Bureau at 1-866-248-3049 or visit our website at www.simonspeakers.com.

Interior design by Wendy Blum

Manufactured in the United States of America

1   3   5   7   9   10   8   6   4   2

Library of Congress Cataloging-in-Publication Data is available.

ISBN 978-1-6680-2510-9
ISBN 978-1-6680-2512-3 (ebook)

MISRECOGNITION

Part

ONE

"**H**ow are you?" Elsa eventually asked.

"I'm fine. How are you?" the woman replied.

Elsa considered the question, turning it over in her mind. She thought of the note her mother had left on the kitchen counter. She looked at the woman seated in the armchair across from her.

"A little off, I guess."

The woman did not respond. Elsa felt the pressure to elaborate, though nothing had changed since the week before. She did not wish to talk about the man and the woman, but she found in the silence that there was nothing else. She had a thought, which produced a feeling.

"I feel like I'm boring you."

"You're not boring me."

Elsa did not reply.

"But what if you were boring me?" the therapist continued. "What then?"

Elsa ignored the question. Her resistance was weak. She began to speak, as she had weeks prior, of the man and the woman, and of her various options as she had come to think of them, though her belief in her ability to shift the course of events was dwindling. The therapist listened intently, nodding as punctuation.

Elsa spoke and the therapist listened, and though she found herself able to discuss—in fits and starts, in circles and tangents—the man and the woman, there were many topics which she could not or did not want to broach with the therapist, such as: her suspicions about the phantom ticking of clocks, or about her perceived ability to map the coursing of blood in her veins, or about the dryness she encountered at the tips of her fingers despite numerous attempts at autostimulation. Nor did she articulate—no matter how much she had been urged in their short time together to share her honest thoughts and feelings about the therapist—the degree to which the cosmetically paralyzed patch between the woman's eyebrows, which induced in the therapist an inability to emote a full range of expression, left her with the sensation that she was speaking to a person whom she could not adequately read. She did not tell the therapist how this made her feel exposed in a situation in which an imbalance of exposure already inhered and was, in fact, the basis for treatment.

Nor did she confess how this frozen patch of muscles, which created a note of discord in the therapist's overall warm demeanor, had a chilling effect to the degree that Elsa herself often left feeling somewhat numb. And she did not allow her therapist to probe at this deflection of blame—of blame for a pervasion of numbness which she felt was to a certain extent caused by the immobilized face of her therapist, a belief which the therapist almost certainly would have questioned—for Elsa did not tell her.

In the midst of discussing the respective merits of her options regarding how to proceed with—or, as seemed increasingly likely, without—the man and the woman, Elsa faltered and grew silent. The constellation of promises that she had pinned upon the man and the woman—mainly, a better life, whatever that meant—had failed to materialize. She could sense herself fumbling toward the desire for new attachments, but had cemented her hopes so solidly on the old ones that it was difficult to envision a future without them.

"The issue is that there's no blueprint for how to live," Elsa said. "Or what to do when your fantasies no longer love you back."

After a brief pause, the therapist put forth the possibility of deferring any action in relation to the man and the woman until further notice. Elsa felt exhausted.

The therapist directed the conversation to a particular event in Elsa's childhood—an event which the two had recently begun to discuss, and which the therapist had, in their last session, gone so far as to deem "traumatic," a word toward which Elsa felt ambivalence, to say the least—and for a fraction of a second, she began to feel the room around her dissolve into tiny particles.

Her vision snapped back into focus. Without responding directly to the therapist's interjection, Elsa continued, "I guess I'm just feeling a lack of optimism. Like, about the possibilities of desire." She stared down at the pillow beside her and began to finger its tasseled edges.

Inside, the house was quiet, though Elsa could hear a faint stirring from her parents' room on the floor above. She had not considered the contours of her day beyond the appointment and so stood staring at the empty kitchen, unsure of what to do next. The note her mother had left for her on the counter was gone.

Elsa started at the flush of the toilet from the hall bathroom next to the entrance behind her. She heard the water from the sink run, heard hands reaching for the bowl of soap, and tiptoed as if in a trance to stand just outside the closed door. Elsa had played similar tricks as a child, and felt the old anticipatory fluttering in her stomach, a smile across her face.

Her mother swung the door open and screamed, bringing her hands to cover her face. Elsa let out a nervous laugh. Her mother dropped a hand to her heart, the other still cupping her cheek.

"You almost gave me a heart attack. I didn't hear you come in."

The two stood in silence.

"You really scared me," her mother said.

Tentative, her mother reached toward Elsa as if to stroke her hair. Just before contact, she let her hand drop slowly to her side.

"Are you okay? How was your appointment?" her mother asked.

"Fine," Elsa said. "Uneventful."

In a gesture whose motivations she could not fully grasp—it felt neither aggressive nor tender, and appeared to stem from that mysterious desire to ape the movements and speech of others—Elsa reached out and touched her mother's head, completing her mother's aborted attempt. Just before her hand touched down, her mother flinched. When Elsa's hand landed on her mother's hair, a hot blush rose up from her mother's neck and moved across her cheeks.

The covers lay strewn about Elsa's ankles near the foot of the bed. A throbbing sensation appeared near her temples, which she prodded with the middle fingers of both hands, feeling it recede under pressure, only to return with a vengeance once her kneading had subsided. Her arms returned to her sides.

Elsa checked her phone. Sixteen notifications, all from a group thread to which she no longer responded, instead participating as silent witness to the musings of friends with whom she continually neglected to keep in touch. Leaving the thread was one option, but she failed to capitalize on it. Instead, she ignored the unsolicited memes, references to popular culture—which, of late, went over her head—and tidbits from her friends' sex lives. She counted the hours in the day before she could reasonably return to bed: thirteen.

Elsa considered the terms of her arrangement at home—its structure, duration, purpose—which, she noted, were vague. Thoughts emerged, which led her back to the man and the woman. She pondered the confluence of events—many dating as far back as childhood—which accumulated in her as a perceived lack of energy or resources. *To lack the energetic resources*, she mused. *To lack resourceful energy*. Unable to carry her contemplation further, she closed her eyes, floated, thumped, felt the familiar fixing around her lungs. She checked her phone. Twelve hours and forty-seven minutes.

She brought a hand down to the waistband of her underwear and felt the slight indentation it had left in her skin overnight. Pushing past the elastic, she began to touch herself. Her gaze moved about the room as she did this, and as she took in each new object, her hand stopped of its own volition. She noticed this some seconds later each time, after which she would inhale and will herself to begin again. Images—not necessarily, or at least not consistently, of a sexual nature—both remembered and imagined appeared in seemingly random succession, as if projected onto a screen near the forefront of her mind, forcing her to pause anew and remind herself to attend to the primary task.

In slow, determined circles Elsa continued. A familiar image surfaced, which she pushed aside. Since the man and the woman, she had become skeptical of her fantasies. She desired new ones, which, like her, refused to come. The split within her grew larger: she watched herself being watched by herself, and eventually grew bored. Against her light-dappled eyelids, she tried to conjure new reels of longing. She lay still and watched the shapes and colors shift.

In swooped the predictable scene: the man inside her, the woman's mouth on Elsa's. She stopped, looked up at the ceiling, and scanned her fantasy repertoire for a different event. The visions that arose were not her own—a girl in a short skirt on an older man's lap, a woman's wet body pressed up against the wall of a shower, a stepmother and her son. Another time, these might have sufficed, but they struck her now as cliché.

When it became clear that there would be no climax, Elsa let her hand fall beside her, rubbing her pointer and middle fingers absentmindedly against her thumb. She stared up at the abstract shapes of the wooden ceiling. Her hand rose to her face and Elsa inhaled, a faint and familiar smell. She had been shocked to discover it on her fingers the first time she had touched the woman—a scent distinctly personal and yet, it appeared, universal, which clung beneath her nails. As she moved through the day, she had found ways to take in its uncanny odor, not wanting it to fade, a tiny thrill. It was like smelling herself, slightly altered.

With her other hand, she reached over to illuminate her phone once more. No new messages, no news.

Why don't you sit between us?" her mother suggested. Elsa was on the narrow cushion of the window seat in the upstairs library. The couch was too small for three, though her mother had crammed herself to one side to make room. Sasha, her parents' golden retriever, lay sprawled at their feet.

"I'm fine here."

It was the first time Elsa had joined them in the library. Her father bent to open the cabinet beneath the bookshelves to reveal the television. They had decided on a movie which had recently come out on various streaming platforms. Though she missed its theatrical run, Elsa had heard it praised by the people she had come to know through the man and the woman. She was surprised that it had been her father who suggested it.

He clicked play. Her mother stood to lower the lights in the hall.

"Can you shut the door?" he asked.

"I have to pee," her mother said. "Can you pause it?"

Her mother walked down the hall without awaiting an answer. The credits opened on zoomed-in images of bronze statues as jaunty piano music played in the background.

"Paul! Will you please pause it," her mother called from behind the bathroom door. It was Elsa's bathroom, but she could lay no claim to it. It was the one closest to the study.

"It's just the opening credits," her father called back.

Elsa watched her father bury his bare foot in the fur of Sasha's exposed belly and rub absentmindedly. The flush of the toilet sounded down the hall. Her mother appeared in the doorframe.

"You couldn't pause it for five seconds?"

"I can rewind if you want. You only missed the credits."

Her mother sat, and Elsa fingered the phone which she had tucked between the window frame and the cushion. She looked out over the sloping lawn that stretched behind the house, golden in the evening light. If she walked far enough over the hill and through the woods, she could reach her old high school. Never once had she commuted that way in all those years.

"It's fine," her mother said.

The film opens on a European bedroom; summer 1983; "somewhere in Northern Italy." Her mother shifted to tuck her legs beneath her.

"Can you turn the volume down?"

"Please don't," Elsa interjected.

Her father ignored her mother's request, silently siding with Elsa. Sasha let out a sigh.

A beautiful boy stands and looks out an upstairs window. *L'usurpateur*, he says in perfect French. A small green car drives into frame.

Elsa's mother bent to reach for her glass of water, took a sip, and placed it back on the carpet. Elsa adjusted the pillow behind her, uncrossed and recrossed her legs.

"Who's that?" her mother asked.

"We're about to find out," her father replied.

"I mean the actor."

"Mom—" Elsa said, a warning.

Her parents fell silent, and Elsa felt herself soften, welcomed the slippage—chiseled features, polyglottery, languid summer days, inherited wealth, boundless time, timeless beauty. The house around them was still but for the hum of the refrigerator downstairs and the faint groan of wood cooling from the heat. Dogs barked in the fields beyond the open window, and Elsa listened to Sasha's heavy breath as she sunk into the time-space of the film, as if into a warm bath, allowing herself to be moved by the lives of others.

Elsa's mother shifted. Half-naked bodies lay in sun and shade, submerged themselves in rivers and pools and Alpine streams. Elsa pictured the swimming hole up the road, how she had swum there as a teenager every summer. Her mother still went every morning, hours before Elsa awoke.

The characters read all day, or play music, sipping fresh apricot juice from the grove behind the house. The boy protagonist buries his head into the young man's swim trunks, taking in his scent. Everyone smokes, indoors and out; Elsa craved a cigarette.

As the film stretched on, in some manner—metaphysical but also material—Elsa *became* the boy protagonist: the listlessness of his confused longings, the tightly drawn string of his evolving desire for another man, the sensuality of his broodiness. It was all her own.

The boy protagonist is sprawled on the couch in rapture across his parents as his mother reads aloud. Elsa looked over to her parents on the couch; neither looked back.

The boy protagonist bikes to an empty café with the man and circles a monument in a deserted square, hurling a confession across the distance. Elsa ached with his desire. The man and the woman threatened at the periphery. In the dim light, out of the corner of her eyes, the outline of her parents: it could almost be them.

Biking along a dirt road, the pair pulls her back. Dark, oblong trees loom in the distance. By the shore of a stream, the boy commits the forbidden—a hand reaching toward another man, a kiss—and finds himself on the other side of possibility; Elsa, too, felt the cathartic surge of limitless potential. She experienced herself split in two; she was in love with the boy, as him.

Her father moved down to the floor beside Sasha and stretched his legs out in front of him; her mother coughed.

At midnight the two men meet on a balcony. The boy protagonist has been counting down the hours. Elsa reached for the cool exterior of her phone. The camera pans from the bed where the men are about to make love to the darkened trees framed by the window of the boy's bedroom; sighs of pleasure and the rustling of bodies sound just out of frame. Aware of her parents' proximity, Elsa turned her head away from the television and gazed out at the fading light behind the hills.

For several heady days, the men's bodies find one another in attics, in darkened bedrooms, in garden archways at night. But the boy protagonist has forgotten that summers end. Not all days stretch so long, not all nights are so warm. He is taught his first lesson in inevitable endings and impossible attachments; a muted understanding of the insolubility of all love filled Elsa, and this epiphany served as a balm, had a mollifying effect. Its truth washed over her as she pushed thoughts of the man and the woman aside.

As the credits rolled over the handsome and tearful face of first heartbreak, it was Elsa's own heart breaking, as well as the hearts of everyone she had ever loved, and even those she had not.

Her father shut off the television. Elsa stood and walked silently to the bathroom down the hall.

"What did you think?" her mother called after her as she shut the latch.

A pale moon hung low in the sky outside the window. It

disappeared as Elsa turned on the light to study herself in the mirror. She had been moved, had felt herself moved, and she suspected that these changes would be made visible. Was there an openness to her eyes, a broadness to her cheeks that had not been there in the days before? She could not be sure, but it seemed quite possible. She ran the tap and wondered if her parents, too, had felt the shift.

A gentle knock at the door startled her.

"Yes?" she replied, splashing water on her face.

"Good night," she heard her father say.

"Good night."

"Thanks for joining us," he said.

"Of course."

In her bedroom, Elsa searched for the film on her laptop. She tried logging on to a streaming platform with one password and then another. Her cursor hovered over the movie. She pressed play and lowered the volume. The film began for a second time, and she watched from start to finish—chiseled features, polyglottery, languid summer days, inherited wealth, boundless time, timeless beauty, transgression, utopic romance, love's inevitable downfall.

It was impossible that the actor himself had not fallen in love with this precise young man, had not experienced the ecstatic fulfillment of this particular lust, had not felt the desperate hue of this exact heartbreak, because through him so, too, had Elsa. She brought a hand up to her face, surprised to feel the moisture that had collected at the corners of her eyes. The tears were shed both for herself and for the boy, as character and actor. She could not fathom the distinction.

When the final credits rolled for a second time over his soft, tearful face, she was overcome by a deep need to comfort him, to love him in her limited capacity, to comprehend the contours of his soul. Elsa fell asleep in the early hours of the morning, her laptop open on her chest. A brief search of its history would have revealed a trail of devoured images, articles, and interviews—both video and written—sketching the life and the recent rise to stardom of the actor-character.

The laptop, having slid off her chest at some point in the night, lay dead and open beside her when she awoke around midday. In the bathroom down the hall, Elsa sat on the toilet and grabbed her phone, which she had placed moments prior on the counter's ledge. On it, she typed the actor's name with two thumbs into the browser, clicked on the third video from the top, and watched as he began a jocular repartee with the host of a popular late-night talk show. She could not remember if this particular interview was one she had seen along with the others the night before, or if it was a new one she had just discovered.

As the actor spoke, she studied his graceful movements, his lanky frame folding in on itself. The composed expressivity of his face and upper limbs belied a certain tension, a libidinal vibration requiring constant vigilance for threat of spilling over. Though he smiled and laughed, she perceived a barely contained wildness in his docility, a slight clenching of the muscles along the sharp line of his jaw. She recognized the same frenetic beauty in the character from the film, and through it, erotic possibility itself.

His words penetrated her thoughts and Elsa felt a discord between the man before her and the one she had come to love the night before. The actor spoke with false humility about the nature of fame. He professed feelings of unworthiness, insisting on his continued status as a "normal guy." He found himself starstruck by the celebrities he increasingly encountered at award ceremonies and their after-parties. He still took the subway! If the words he uttered were banal, Elsa believed it was merely evidence of his soul's refusal to engage in the undignified circus of fame, even if his body must.

Elsa put the phone down and looked out the window, picturing the man and the woman, and a time when there had been a kind of optimism to her coasting. She envied the character from the film the purity of his expression, envied the actor for the same reason, and noted that even in certain instances when she was undeniably an active participant in the unfolding of her life, she couldn't shake the feeling of being a person to whom things happened, rather than one who incited their occurrence.

She realized that she was someone who believed deeply, to the point of superstition, that the more one longed for something, the more this sealed one's fate and ensured its non-occurrence. Like advancing toward a mirage, approaching an object headlong merely ensured its dissolution.

Instead, Elsa had learned to focus laterally on tertiary interests and let luck have its way. This refusal of the pursuit of desire had once seemed to her a kind of higher state, a practice of non-attachment. She preferred to let the chips fall where they may, thereby imbuing the void with meaning, as if her life were predetermined by an unseen yet overpowering force. Like God, but not quite. Now she was not so sure. She got off the toilet.

For the rest of the day, she carried the actor-character inside her. Though she loved the young man, Elsa was aware that this love was dependent on the actor-character's love for men—explicit in the character, implicit in the performance of the actor—and of the impossibility of love in general. She could not love a heterosexual man—that is to say, one who could love her back—so purely and without reserve. *Such is the nature of desire*, she thought.

As she checked her email, as she listened for the sound of a car pulling out of the driveway before leaving her room and making her way downstairs to the kitchen, as she made herself a breakfast of two shots of espresso with cream at nearly one in the afternoon, she did so as some combination of herself and the boy. His presence had enveloped her like a second skin.

A printed résumé lay on the passenger seat as Elsa pulled out of the dirt drive and made a left toward town. The night before, she had searched and finally discovered an old copy, emailed to herself years ago. Her address and contact information had been updated to reflect her new situation. Notably absent was her time at the gallery and the studio, so as not to evoke the man and the woman or be forced to explain their strange situation. As the fields passed on either side, she contemplated how to account for the two-year gap on her résumé if it should be brought to her attention. She wondered if it mattered. It was only a coffee shop.

At the roundabout, signs on the green announced the programming for the town's summer theater festival. Elsa pictured people from the city—what had been her city for the past seven years, but which now appeared, even in her imagination, foreign and inhospitable—flocking to the rural town to take in culture and spot the few celebrities who had been cast this season. A photograph she had seen on one of her social platforms a few years prior arose in her mind: her friend from middle school standing with her arm around a handsome movie star. Elsa recalled being struck by the proximity and juxtaposition of these two faces, which were each familiar and known to her, though in vastly different ways. It had taken her a moment to realize she was looking at the image of a former friend in the presence of an intimate stranger. The star had gone to the deli, owned by her friend's parents, to get a sandwich.

Elsa drove and thought of the strange familiar-unfamiliar quality of the famous. Once she reached the town's single street of commerce, she parallel parked, locked the car, and entered the coffee shop.

There were three people in line. As new patrons entered, Elsa feigned indecision and offered her place to them, so as to delay the inevitable encounter. When, finally, there was no one behind or in front of her, Elsa had no choice but to approach the counter. A girl who appeared sixteen smiled and asked her what she'd like.

"Is there a manager I can speak to?" Elsa asked.

The girl turned to a man in his twenties behind the espresso machine.

"Is Toby still in the back?"

"I'm not sure, but you can check," the man replied. He turned to Elsa and asked if there was something he could help her with.

"Oh. I don't know," Elsa said. "I'm looking for a job."

"I'll go see if I can find Toby," the girl offered sweetly, and made her way through the rubber swinging doors into what Elsa assumed was the kitchen.

"Thanks," Elsa remembered to say, too late to be heard.

More people entered and gave their requests to the man, who was now stationed at the register. Elsa moved to the side of the counter where the lids were stacked. The barista smiled at her occasionally as he took and fulfilled drink orders, and she tried effortfully to return the gesture.

A slim, slightly balding man emerged from the back, followed by the girl, who indicated Elsa to him before returning to the till.

"I'm Toby," the man said, reaching out a hand to Elsa.

She took it and noted that she had not been touched by a stranger since—she could not recall. The familiar tingling sensation reappeared, and Elsa ignored the impulse to pull back as if from a hot surface. "Elsa," she said, as he released his grip.

"Why don't we sit over here."

He led her to a small wooden table nearby. Once the two were seated, the man asked if she had a résumé on her and, as she retrieved the document from her bag, if she had ever worked "in coffee."

"No, but I've worked in hospitality," she replied, handing her résumé over to him. "I used to host at a restaurant." She reminded herself to smile.

"I see." He glanced at the paper before him and then back up at Elsa. "Is this up-to-date?"

"Yes," she said, noting the flatness in her voice. She was aware of the tingling sensation in her hands.

"I only ask because it seems the last job you held was over two years ago."

"Right."

The two exchanged a long silence. Elsa fought the urge to escape the man's gaze.

"I worked informally for a few friends in the interim, but it didn't seem relevant."

He raised his eyebrows in what appeared to Elsa mock intrigue.

"Relevant to what?" he asked.

"To working at a coffee shop."

Elsa regretted coming.

"What sort of work, if you don't mind my asking? Off the record."

He winked at her. She was unable to determine if this was sarcasm or a genuine attempt at camaraderie.

"For friends, mostly. Artists." She was stumbling. "Like an artist's assistant, kind of." The end of the statement rose in inflection, as if it were a question.

"Were you paid for this work?"

Elsa thought of the man and the woman and of their particular situation—of the gallery downtown and the studio in Greenpoint—and deliberated for a moment before continuing. "My expenses were taken care of, yes."

The man called Toby smiled and nodded in friendly acknowledgment to a person somewhere beyond Elsa's shoulder before returning to her résumé.

"I see your last job—well, your last official job," he said, looking up at her and grinning cryptically, "was in New York."

"Correct."

"And have you been living there or here since?"

Elsa thought of Frieze London and the Bienal de São Paulo and of Art Basel. She thought of the correspondences she had sent on behalf of the gallery (the woman) and the artist (the man), and of schedules managed and fairs booked and of menial tasks, but also ones of great importance: the organization of installs, the booking of travel, the freighting of artworks across seas. And then Caro's couch after the breakup.

"Um, a little bit all over the place, actually," she replied.

Elsa glanced over her shoulder and wondered if it might be possible to get up from the table and simply walk out the door.

"My apologies if I'm boring you with all my questions."

Elsa turned back to the man called Toby as he placed the résumé face down between them on the table, and felt a heat rise to her face.

"Not at all."

As their eyes met, she felt the particles of dust dissipate, her mind blown clean for an instant, and wondered if something had shifted. She surveyed the surrounding tables and felt the fog roll back in, thick and steady. The two looked at one another in silence across the table. It was a void Elsa could not, in her present condition, fill.

"Well, it's been nice chatting with you," he said. "We're not currently hiring for someone with no barista experience, but I'll let you know if we get desperate." He lifted her résumé with him as he rose from his seat. "Mind if I hold on to this?"

"Of course," Elsa replied.

She stood to take his outstretched hand. The man called Toby shook it curtly and turned his back on her, making his way across the space and disappearing into the kitchen.

As Elsa left the coffee shop from the side entrance and walked out onto the small lawn scattered with wooden picnic tables, her eyes traveled to a group seated near the sidewalk at a round table in the sun. There was nothing ostentatious in their dress, and she might otherwise have overlooked them, but something about how the disparate parts of the group fit together, the manner in which each individual held their body, drew her attention to the small crowd. A man sat with his back to Elsa, and she felt the collective energy of the table direct itself toward him, as if each person were somehow connected to him by an invisible thread. She could not make out his features, but she, too, felt the pull.

Though her car was in the opposite direction, she found herself walking past the table and down to the sidewalk, as if impelled, turning left when she should have turned right. The air around her stilled as she neared. She sensed the pulsing of her blood, a tingling in her limbs. Elsa glanced over her shoulder and was overtaken by a feeling of déjà vu, as if experiencing the resurfacing of an intimate memory, long forgotten. Which is to say, she both knew this man and did not know him.

Elsa rounded the corner of the lawn and turned to look at the group once more. Seated at the table was the actor from the movie. It was by his hands that she first recognized him, their delicate grip on the empty plastic cup, the way he swirled it absentmindedly, the leftover ice rattling as he spoke. A person to his right grabbed the actor's forearm, and Elsa felt the shock of touch as if it had been her own. The person who had reached out and touched him had a slim frame, visible beneath a simple, oversized T-shirt. Their hair was dark, choppy, and longer at the nape of the neck, where Elsa glimpsed a silver chain. She looked again at the hands of the actor-character. The person beside him loosened their grip.

Elsa continued down the empty sidewalk, no longer aware of her destination. She wandered away, pausing only once she had turned the corner and was hidden from sight behind the large building which housed the college's indoor track. Her breathing slowed and her vision returned as she lingered in the shade. A thick line of ants hurried along a crack in the sidewalk. After counting to twenty, she began to retrace her steps. She crossed the street and walked toward her mother's parked car.

A thought occurred to her as she put the keys into the ignition and backed out of the spot. She ignored it, but it occurred again, this time with the force of compulsion. As her plan solidified, she experienced the thought that she was perhaps a genius, which was instantaneously followed and supplanted—so as to appear almost simultaneous with the first thought—by the impression that she was destined for failure. She glanced at her hands on the steering wheel to steady herself; she did not recognize them as her own. Were they those of the actor-character? She felt the touch of the person beside him, a hand on her forearm.

E lsa sped up the slight incline of the driveway and ran inside the house.

"Where's Sasha?" she asked as she entered the study.

Her mother turned in her chair.

"What's the matter?" her mother said, her face darkening with concern.

"Nothing's the matter. Where's Sasha?"

Elsa attempted to hide her impatience so as not to raise her mother's permanent state of suspicion.

"How should I know? What do you want her for?"

Elsa turned and began to call for the dog. Her mother stood and followed her into the entryway.

"Elsa, what's the matter?" Her mother scanned her face. "What could you possibly want with Sasha?" she asked.

"I want to take her for a walk," Elsa shot back, before bounding up the stairs, yelling the dog's name as she did.

Elsa found Sasha asleep, her tail and hind legs poking out from under her parents' bed.

"Sasha," Elsa whispered, as she poked the dog's haunches with her foot. The dog lay unmoving.

"Sasha," she tried again, louder this time, and shook her more forcefully.

When the animal gave no signs of life, Elsa bent down to grab her hind legs and dragged the dog gently across the wooden floor and out from underneath the bed. Sasha eventually stood and looked up at Elsa with what she perceived was immense fatigue.

"Come on," Elsa said, raising her voice as if speaking to a small child, guiding the dog toward the door by the collar, until Sasha began to follow of her own accord.

"We're going on an adventure."

In the driveway, Sasha stared blankly at the open hatchback trunk, ignoring Elsa's commands to get in. Elsa bent down and lifted the dog's front paws, tipping her into the back.

As Elsa sped into town, she glanced every so often in her rearview mirror to check that the dog was still there. She felt a pang of guilt every time her eyes found Sasha's soft golden head resting in obedient anticipation over the top of the back seat.

She parked once again in the lot at the base of the street. When she opened the trunk, Sasha leapt out and Elsa bent to secure the leash. She led her across the asphalt toward the café, the dog's tail wagging excitedly. A few people stopped them on their way, asking if they could pet her. Elsa waited, basking in the certainty of her plan's success.

As she rounded the corner of the coffee shop's exterior, she spotted the group at the same table, though the palpable aura which had previously emanated from them had since grown faint. Elsa slowed, feeling the leash grow taught as Sasha continued on. Her eyes traveled seamlessly among the seated bodies, as if over a single unit. No detail called out to her, only the absence of tension. Sasha moved further, and Elsa followed, searching the bodies for the tall, slender back, somewhat hunched, for the delicate hands, but perceived instead a lacuna in the forcefield. The man was missing.

She faltered at the edge of the grass.

"Sit, Sasha," she said. The dog ignored her.

An older couple sat in the sun, dressed as if for a colder month, in khaki pants and long-sleeved, pastel shirts. Matching wide-brimmed hats hid their faces from view, their heads bowed in silence as they read the paper. Sasha pulled at the lead and Elsa looked around for the actor-character. Perhaps he had gone to the bathroom. A man in the group laughed and threw his head back. The person who had been beside the actor-character moved to stand, their hand resting gently on the shoulder of a woman.

Sasha strained toward the group, harder this time, and though Elsa felt the urge to flee, she allowed herself to be dragged in their direction.

Sasha began to sniff the leg of the person with the silver chain, who gasped and turned, crouching to pet the dog. Elsa took a step back, as far as the leash would allow, and began to usher an apology, but the thought failed to complete itself.

"Sweet boy," they said.

Elsa did not correct them; she had little stake in Sasha's gender. Instead, she studied the person's bent figure, the lean musculature of their arms, the place between their brows where soft, dark hairs met. They looked up at Elsa and smiled. Their eyes were a soft brown flecked with green, kinder than Elsa had anticipated. They appeared on the verge of speech, but a handsome man interrupted.

"And who is this cutie?" he asked, squatting to allow Sasha to lick his face.

Elsa felt the question was rhetorical, and so did not answer, though she took a step closer. Sasha quivered excitedly, her tail wagging. Those who were seated turned their affections to the dog, though never to Elsa, and she stood and watched as they cooed and patted, and felt her face grow hot, though she reminded herself that no one was looking. She scanned the lawn for the actor-character, but he appeared to be definitively absent from the landscape.

Sasha wriggled away from the group, leading Elsa down toward the sidewalk, her nose to the ground, moving in zigzags across the grass in pursuit of some novel scent. Elsa dumbly waved a half-hearted farewell, though she could not be sure that anyone had noticed.

The dog pulled Elsa onto the sidewalk and lowered her haunches to pee. Elsa had not thought past this point of the plan. Tugging Sasha's leash, she turned with feigned purpose in the opposite direction and up the main street. The dog followed reluctantly at first, but soon began to trot in front of her. A fatigue came over her, totalizing in a way she had not experienced since the blurred weeks that followed the rupture, and before that, never in her life.

Her blood slowed its pumping, the tingling in her hands relaxed its grip, her legs grew heavy. She walked past the bookstore, past the small white building in which she revealed weekly—though more reservedly, she believed, than her therapist would like—her inner life, and past the liquor store on the opposite side, where she had purchased cigarettes less than a week ago. In her bedroom remained half a pack; she wished for one now. Reaching the top of the street, she turned around. As she made her way back down to her mother's car, she spotted the person whom Sasha had accosted, accompanied by the actor-character.

In later reflections, Elsa would struggle to recall her continued trajectory toward the pair. The two approached her, their arms nearly touching, or so she believed. Both wore sunglasses—of that Elsa would find herself certain.

Sasha ignored them and Elsa nodded at the person beside the actor-character, who nodded back in recognition, their head tilted slightly toward the actor-character, listening as he spoke. Elsa found she could not look at him, keeping her gaze on the person beside him instead. As their bodies passed, Elsa felt the blood rush to her face and turned to look into the shop window beside her, startled by the verisimilitude of two mannequins, a man and a small child, who crouched in the display, dressed head to toe in the paraphernalia of the town's college. For an instant she had believed them real.

To what degree the actor-character had registered her, she could not have said. She would mull this event over in the days to come, spinning it both ways: she had not been noticed at all; the actor-character had felt himself overcome by desire. She wondered if the two were a couple, the actor-character and the person who had grabbed his forearm, who had accompanied him, alone, up the street.

When she arrived at the car, she unlocked the doors, helped Sasha into the trunk, and lowered herself into the driver's seat, finding her phone inside her bag. She typed the actor's name into the search engine, along with the name of her town. She scrolled past unrelated articles until she found the theater festival's website. The actor was to star in a play this summer. He would be spending the season in her hometown.

E lsa typed a message into her phone, redacting and rewriting, often to type the precise phrasing she had deleted seconds earlier. She read the text over, double-tapped her phone to select all, and deleted the message in its entirety, which had taken her over thirty minutes to compose. Typing anew, she rashly hit send, as if some ulterior hand had moved her own equivocal one. She read her message: *Can we talk? Pleas respond.* The missing *e* flaunted itself. It was an intrusion on the few instances of forgetful calm she experienced throughout the day as she awaited a response from the woman.

By nightfall, all hope of a reply had been extinguished. Elsa threw her phone onto the chair, no longer tethered to its consequence. She pictured her bank account, its digits descending. They would soon reach zero if she continued to forestall an intervention. She thought, briefly, of the man named Toby at the coffee shop, and then of her unanswered text and the missing "e." It was difficult not to feel that had she typed "please" instead of "pleas," things might have turned out differently.

Seated on the roof, she brought a cigarette to her mouth and then let it hang limply from her outstretched hand, her wrist balanced on her knee. What would the actor-character do in her position? She concluded that he would have sent the message, but believed he would have fretted over it less, his spelling nevertheless impeccable, the verbiage less clichéd. *Can we talk?* The phrase circled in her mind until it had rid itself of meaning. Perhaps his gesture would have been grander, perhaps he would have shown up in person, not taken no for an answer. Elsa was aware of the futility of her desires; she knew better than to commit such an act. Instead, she restricted herself to meager attempts at reconciliation, her pleas unanswered.

Before sleep, she thought of the actor-character and began to touch herself, the tips of her fingers on her hip. Her motions were languid, noncommittal, as if seducing something skittish within herself. She felt the hairs on the tops of her thighs, which turned into coarser ones as she moved in closer. Disparate images played before her—some from the film, others from their brief encounter, and others still from an imagined future. Settling on one, she noted an absence of tension, causing a minor disturbance to flare up inside her, but she rode the feeling toward its dissolution.

The actor-character finds her sleeping. The actor-character touches her softly, so as to arouse without rousing. The actor-character patiently works until he feels her grow wet, pausing only then to remove his clothes. The actor-character returns to the bed, hovering above her before he slides inside her, his skin warm and smooth. Relieved of the burden of articulated desires, she drifts in a state between wakefulness and sleep. She is pliant and yielding; he handles fantasy and action for them both. She feels herself pulled by the hips onto him over and over again, a steady motion, dependable.

Elsa felt the blood travel from her brain and flow downward, giving over to its pulse and swell. She began to falter as images threatened to appear: of blood pumping, of clocks ticking, of texts unanswered.

But the actor-character keeps these thoughts at bay, rocking her from within, enveloping her in his embrace, his entire weight pressed upon her.

Her breath caught as she came.

The next morning, Elsa dimly recalled an arm extended in search of contact, an abrupt awakening, like falling; the discovery of a void, her hand tracing the bedsheets beside her, empty and cool; an apprehension of solitude, like fate, airtight and complete.

Each day, Elsa drove to the coffee shop, the initial site of contact. She ignored the pangs of hunger she knew would soon dissipate and was halfway to town before she came into awareness of herself and the certainty of her destination. She would purchase a coffee, a cortado with half-and-half (she could not bring herself to say *breve*), and wander about the café, as if awaiting a tardy companion.

She would remain suspended in a state of dreadful anticipation, experiencing each time the eventual confirmation of the actor-character's absence as relief. She could never discern how long she stood waiting. In these moments, she experienced the simultaneous quickening and slowing of time so that she found herself unaware of its passing and yet each instant, imbued with tense expectancy, was acutely felt.

Twice, she saw the person who had accompanied the actor-character as they walked up the street, the one who had smiled at her. Whenever she spotted them, Elsa experienced a hopeful foreboding, but the person appeared always alone and never to recognize Elsa.

E lsa reached for her laptop and began to search the internet. After a cursory glance at a major news outlet—the same site that had sent recipe suggestions to her phone earlier that day—she found herself on a popular entertainment platform, scrolling through the promoted content. Her cursor came to rest on a show for which, the platform's algorithm told her, she was a 97 percent match. The show had aired over three years ago. Elsa pictured her data and tried to recall what programs she had watched, and in what sequence. She tried to map her viewing habits: Which shows had she binged, and which ones had she savored? Which shows had she abandoned, sometimes in the middle of the first episode, and to which shows had she loyally returned? She found she could not re-create the vague patterns of her entertainment consumption—an accumulation of far too many hours—and felt some relief at the thought that even if she could not extract sense or order from the unmemorable trail of her ennui, at least someone was keeping track.

Elsa clicked on the recommended show and lay down on her back, her laptop resting on her stomach.

A black minivan parks outside a single-story family home somewhere in the southwestern United States. A petite Japanese woman steps out of the car. She is dressed neatly in a cream cardigan, a purple pleated skirt, and black tights with matching black ballet flats. As she approaches the house, the woman is accompanied by someone who appears to be her assistant, a younger woman dressed in a black blazer and matching slacks. The assistant trails the woman, scurrying with an arm outstretched to hold up an oversized umbrella attempting to shield them both from the light rain. Two smiling white Americans—a man and a woman—greet them at the door, a young child resting on each of their hips. The assistant turns out to be the woman's translator. The Japanese woman is introduced to both family and audience as a "tidying expert." She is there to instill order, to wipe away the messiness of their lives. The husband and wife are young and attractive; they call each other "babe." They are the perfect couple. The camera cuts to confessionals of husband and wife, shot separately, as they lay out for an unseen interviewer how the task of organizing the overwhelming number of material things in their lives has taken a toll on their ability to love, to be good parents, to be patient spouses. They are tearful. They need a change.

Elsa felt the warm laptop on her stomach and thought briefly of radiation. She noted with little fanfare that she no longer clung to the ensurance of her own survival. She left the laptop where it was.

The expert kneels on the carpet of the living room floor while the couple sits in matching oversized stuffed gray armchairs, a child nestled into each of their laps. A framed print on the wall between them reads in cursive *Bless this house with love and laughter*. The kneeled expert asks, through her translator, if she may thank the house. Once permission has been granted, she closes her eyes in prayer, her hands touching palm-to-palm in front of her chest, the tips of her fingers just below her chin. After a few moments of heavy silence, she bows, touching her forehead to the floor. The children have fallen asleep in the calm of their parents' arms.

Elsa laid an absentminded palm across her heart.

The expert orders the couple to empty out their closets, their bureau drawers. The couple keeps their clothing stored in separate rooms. The wife takes her articles and piles them high on the bed. When confronted with the sight of so many things, she is embarrassed and attests to a feeling of guilt. She thinks—aloud, briefly—of how much she has compared to those who have so little. But time is of the essence, and she is not left to dwell on the thought. She is told by the expert via translator to take each item in hand, to really feel it, and if it sparks joy, keep it; if it elicits no feeling whatsoever, the wife must sincerely thank the item for its service, and then dispose of it. When there is confusion over what it means, precisely, to "spark joy," the expert squinches her eyes shut, bringing two tiny fists up beside her smiling cheeks, and says in unsteady English, "like all your cells are rising." Her eyes pop open to look at the couple, beaming.

Elsa noted that her own cells had been dormant for some time.

The couple has been fighting about laundry. The expert insists that folding is an important opportunity to convey love to one's clothes. By running one's palm over each item, by smoothing out the creases, by folding it properly, one is displaying one's gratitude for its service. The couple is taught to fold shirts first, then pants. When the expert reveals the results of each—a rolled, tent-like structure, rigid enough to stand on its own—there is genuine wonderment on their faces. The children clap.

And just like that, the expert and her assistant depart, promising to check in on them soon. Alone, the couple surveys the detritus in stunned silence.

The next day, there is an argument about hangers—the wife does not want to throw away the surplus. She is in the midst of explaining that it's a waste to dispose of them, that she doesn't see why they can't store them in the garage, when the husband shouts back from the threshold of their shared bedroom, "Do they spark joy?" The wife starts to protest, but the husband cuts in, "A bin full of hangers brings you joy?" Joy has become a weapon, an abstraction they hold over one another.

The threat of joy, Elsa thought to herself.

A week later, the tidying expert returns to the family home, this time armed with boxes for miscellaneous items. She explains in sub-titled Japanese, speaking directly into the camera, that miscellaneous items include anything outside the primary categories of clothing, books, documents, and sentimental items. In her hands she holds boxes of various sizes stacked neatly inside one another. "By using boxes, you can compartmentalize."

Elsa looked down at her forearms and watched the fine hairs rise.

"While you are tidying, it may seem like things are more cluttered than before," the expert says, staring directly into the camera from the anesthetized stage set. "But there's no need to worry. By follow-ing the process step-by-step, there will always be an end to tidying."

Elsa felt a strange tingling in her eyes and nose. She drew her middle finger up to trace her lower lashes. When she brought her hand down to the mattress, circling her finger gently across the pad of her thumb, she noted a hint of moisture. She closed the laptop.

O nce her parents had gone to bed, Elsa opened the window of her bedroom and climbed out onto the roof of the porch that jutted out from the side of the house. The moon was full and lit up the lawn before her, the trees casting long shadows across the recently mown grass, its sweet odor discernible even at her height. She felt into her pack of cigarettes and withdrew one, her fifth of the day. As she lit it and inhaled, she was aware that in another period of her life, a moment such as this—the moonlit cigarette, the early summer night, the black outline of the mountain in the distance—would have held a kind of romance for her. She might have watched herself smoking from some other vantage point, might have felt the strange sensation of being both embodied and outside herself, a spectator of her existence. She coughed out smoke instead.

Her phone lay inside and she felt the urge to check it, but she picked instead at the splintered wood of the slats beneath her. She thought of the couple who had been saved by the expert, and of how sometimes baggage is more than just a metaphor. Feeling the man and the woman enter her thoughts, she took another drag of the cigarette and watched the tip enflame.

She took a final inhale and stubbed it out, leaving a smudge of ash. The nicotine rushed to her head as she stood and ducked beneath the window and onto the empty desk. Hopping down to the floor, she walked directly to her dresser.

Reaching first for her sock drawer, Elsa began to toss its contents onto the bed. Once the rest of her dresser was empty, she did the same to her closet. She stared at the mound. Grabbing the nearest article—a cream silk blouse she had owned for years—she held it in her hands and rubbed the fabric between her fingers. She felt nothing; she brought the shirt up to her face and buried her nose in its folds, taking in the stale musk of her childhood closet. She thought of the actor-character, how he had buried his head into the man's bathing suit. Elsa threw the shirt on the ground. As if in a trance, she did the same with each item, until the entirety of her material belongings lay strewn on the floor, a moat surrounding the bed. She had lost track of time; she checked her phone; it was past midnight.

The heap of clothes gave Elsa a momentary glimmer of hope. She stood motionless. A minute, perhaps two, passed, and she found she could not carry the impulse further. She had briefly envisioned an alternate path for herself, picturing the line of bags to be donated on the couple's kitchen floor. But the thrill subsided, and thoughts filled her head like a heavy weight. She bent down tentatively to pick up a gray shirt from the top of the pile, running her hands across it the way the expert had. She pictured sending love to the item. Folding the shirt in the manner of the expert, she laid it to one side.

The hours passed as Elsa stroked her clothes, folding and tucking them neatly into place. When she was finished, it was close to two in the morning. She opened her drawer to stare at her handiwork, running her fingers along the color-coded bands that stood neatly at attention. She grabbed her phone to take a picture and pressed the box with the arrow on the lower left-hand side of the screen. She clicked on the message button and a text box arose with her neatly folded clothes inside it. Her thumbs hovered for a moment as she considered the blank line at the top. She could think of no recipient.

As she drove the sleepy two-lane highway, past the apple orchards on the right and the fields of unmown grass on the left, Elsa thought of the couple from the show and their surplus of things. She pictured her own objects, not many, stored away inside her childhood dresser and closet, and wondered where the material items of her youth had gone—likely donated over time by her mother, or in storage bins in the attic. She drove past the bakery, midway into town, its A-frame structure and pastel exterior lending it a small-town quaintness, and wished for more clutter, a mess on a grand scale, so as to make conspicuous her predicament.

Inside the restaurant, Elsa sat across the table from the manager in the empty dining room. A white tablecloth lay on the table between them. Elsa studied the manager's skin (bare) and hair (blond, also natural, or so it appeared to Elsa), the gentle slope of her nose, which rose at the tip, as the woman read Elsa's résumé on her lap, head bent. Elsa sat up straight, her hands clasped together on the table. She had not been there since her high-school graduation. The interview was short, and at its conclusion, the woman asked if she was free to come in on Thursday.

As Elsa made her way down the steep path to the parking lot, she felt a lightness in her step which recalled the time before; the remembrance incurred a deflation. She opened the door to her mother's car and sat for a moment before starting the engine. Elsa checked her phone. A text from Caro, asking if she could come visit. She put the device away.

Thursday came, and Elsa carried throughout the day an unfamiliar sense of anticipation, of having a particular place to be at a given time. She counted down the hours, touching her phone periodically to check the time, and when she dressed, she was thankful she had not disposed of all her clothes, though the desire had nearly engulfed her. She found hanging in her closet a pair of old trousers and paired them with a silk blouse. On her way to the car, she noted a shift in the manner she carried herself, her gait hopeful and quick, as she hurried down the steps, her mother's car keys clinking gently in her hand.

When she arrived at the restaurant, the manager introduced her to a man named Max and quickly disappeared into the restaurant's interior, leaving the two alone in the lobby. Max began his various opening tasks, narrating each step to Elsa until they were complete. Elsa followed closely behind, nodding along without truly listening, her head tilted in feigned concentration as her attention wandered over and over to the glass door and the summer afternoon beyond. When guests began to arrive, Elsa trailed Max as he led them into the dining room. She peered over his shoulder when they returned to the front desk, to watch him record on the iPad where each party had been seated. He repeated the table numbers frequently, looking at her eagerly as he did so, as if checking her comprehension. Elsa smiled stiffly. Though she knew it to be critical information if she were to take the job, she could not will herself quite yet to learn the layout of the dining room.

In periods of downtime, Elsa was grateful for Max's lack of interest in her. He spoke in monologue and required little participation apart from the occasional and vaguely encouraging remark. Elsa began to notice the way her language repeated itself, as she heard herself say *right* more times than she could count and laughed thinly. Her thoughts began to drift toward the man and the woman, and then the actor-character, Max's voice a backdrop to her contemplation. Though she longed to look at her phone, Max hadn't looked at his once, and so she resisted the urge to retrieve hers from the bag which hung inside the coat closet.

The rest of the evening passed slowly, and when the manager came by to release her, Elsa told her that she would take the job, if they would have her. After five hours of feeling its absence, she pulled her phone out on her way down to her car; she had no notifications. She could not have said from whom she had expected to hear, but the return to the outside world had ushered in a state of anticipation, and she suffered the letdown all the more acutely.

The next day, Elsa received an email from the manager with a link. She clicked and was taken to a site where she entered her address and social security number, number of dependents (0), secondary job (none), along with the routing and account numbers for her bank, and felt herself shift, with some ambivalence, into the realm of the employed.

" I texted her," Elsa said.

When the therapist asked for clarification, uttering the woman's name—as in, the woman as opposed to the man—Elsa nodded in assertion.

"And have you heard back?" the therapist asked.

"No." Elsa resisted the urge to reach into her bag and check her phone.

"And how do you feel, not having received a response?"

Elsa considered a moment. She replied, "It feels like reality sinking to the level of my expectations."

The therapist gave the impression that, had her eyebrows been mobile, she would have raised them at the disclosure.

"There's some comfort in things not working out," Elsa added.

"Do you believe that history equals destiny?" her therapist asked.

"Did you know I haven't dreamt once since I've been home?"

"Not once?" the therapist replied, smiling to indicate that she would, for the time being, indulge the diversion.

"Not that I can recall," Elsa said.

"And does this concern you?" the therapist asked.

"Does it concern *you*?"

The therapist paused and her gaze traveled to the corner of the room past Elsa's head.

"Not really," she said finally, shrugging for casual emphasis.

"I thought therapists loved dreams."

Though she tried, Elsa could not stop a smile from forming. The therapist let out a laugh.

"Well, you're not giving me very much to work with here." The therapist turned her hands so that they lay palm up in her lap, an open gesture. "If you remember any in the future, by all means—"

"Oh, also. I got a job."

The woman had not replied, and so had in a way freed her from at least one of her options. Elsa checked her phone. A notification alerted her that the company that owned two of the three social media platforms she visited daily was releasing a new cryptocurrency. She considered how this might affect her life and decided that in the immediate term, like most world events, the answer was not at all.

As she lay in the semidarkness of her room, the small glow of her phone's screen illuminated her face. She liked and then unliked a post; she let the stories play, one after another, without skipping through the ads. It was comforting, she thought, as a promotional video for an online workout subscription played on her screen, that her phone thought her still capable of or interested in such things. Clicking on the profile, she read the bio: *a research-based and results-proven fitness methodology for total balance in the body.* Photos of a petite blonde in ab-exposing workout gear populated the grid; Elsa clicked back to her stories.

Strangers and old friends appeared before her. More ads, this time for a sustainable fashion brand. She thought of the gestures, mostly subconscious, she performed daily across her various devices that created a kind of intimacy, determining which ads might one day appear on this same handheld screen, or one very much like it. These ads, curated specifically for her, would reflect back to Elsa her identity—or at least the parts projected into cyberspace through the accounts she followed, the items she purchased with whatever currency, the sorts of things she searched for—and would go on to inform this identity, as some algorithmic version of what she had once liked would subtly shape her future self, persuading her of who she had been and who she might still become.

Elsa searched for the profile of the man. She did not click the circular photo on the upper left-hand corner of his profile, which she knew would reveal photographs and videos uploaded by the man with the intent of their disappearance. One's *story*, as the platform called it, toggled, as in life, perpetually between proclamation, erasure, and revision.

Had she been able to consume such images anonymously, she would have looked and re-looked, until the photos and videos faded from public existence. Elsa felt the compulsion to click ripple through her like nausea but let the feeling pass, believing the indulgence of that particular urge to lie beyond a limit which, if crossed, might contaminate her life by ridding it of its already dwindling sense of containment.

Instead, she checked the most recently posted photographs on the man's profile to verify that no changes had occurred. She then searched for the name of the actor and glided through a seemingly infinite stream of photos, her thumb moving in steady strokes. Stills from the film mixed with images of the actor posing on red carpets or seated on unmemorable talk-show sofas, which only furthered Elsa's suspicions that to separate the actor from the character was akin to attempting to extricate one's soul from one's body.

Her screen appeared black before her; she had clicked the story on the actor's profile. Turning up the volume, she realized she was watching a video—a video of darkness, of nothing—as a song began to play through her phone's small speakers. She recognized the track but had not thought of it for some time, and felt herself briefly transported to a southern state, driving past palm trees, through suburban time with an ex, before the man or the woman, hundreds of miles from her current predicament. The actor-character had likely been listening to this song not so far from where she now lay in bed. She had a thought, which she pushed away. The thought resurfaced. She watched the video once more, a blank canvas in negative. *I wonder if he's alone*, she thought. Another version might have been: *I wonder if he's lonely.*

Elsa typed in the name of the woman. The familiar images failed to appear; in their stead was black text against a white background which read "No Posts Yet," below a stencil drawing of a camera inside a circle. She refreshed the page. The outcome was the same. Her laptop lay on the floor beside her bed, and she reached for it, typing the woman's name and clicking on the link to the same profile. She had not logged on to this device, and as an anonymous user she was able to view the images: photos of the woman, things and people the woman had seen, images which constituted, for Elsa, familiar landmarks and the passage of time. She scrolled until she reached the two photos, one next to the other, which bore record, invisible to the uninvested eye, to the definitive existence of a *before* and *after*.

The woman had blocked her.

Elsa reopened the app on her phone and searched her own profile. She scrolled through her posts, down past photos of the man and the woman, down further past images of friends to whom she no longer spoke and lovers she no longer loved, all the way to the beginning. Perhaps she had been perpetually reading the story in reverse. Whatever the crucial turning point, whatever the moment it had all gone awry, she might discover it now, if only she began at square one. Her first post: a picture of her, smiling from a sunny rooftop, her arm around a woman she no longer knew. The photos rose before her in sequence as she scrolled slowly upward, this time as the actor-character, allowing the context of each new image to elude her, and felt herself slip into his presence.

The static noise of her own subjectivity had long overwhelmed her, and she wished to observe herself as the actor-character might. When she at last reached the end of the sequence—her most recent post, which might have otherwise indicated its starting point to a newcomer—she felt no clearer on who she had been and who she might become. She wondered if the actor-character would find her pretty.

Elsa walked to the bathroom to pee. She stood before the mirror to study her features.

C aro arrived late Friday night. The two assessed one another as they withdrew from their embrace by the front door. Caro's bag sat on the threshold between them. Her *best friend*. The notion struck Elsa as childish, but she could think of no better term. She felt overexposed beneath the hall's light fixture, aware of the stiffness in her motions which contrasted the ease with which Caro hugged her, stroked her hair, said, searching her features with an earnestness that Elsa could hardly bear, "How are you?"

Elsa had taken comfort in moving through her days mostly undetected; the weekend with Caro stretched before her.

"I'm okay." She shrugged, taking a step back. "How are you?"

"Oh, you know," Caro said.

Elsa realized she didn't. Perhaps for the first time since they had met.

Her parents descended the stairs followed by Sasha, who greeted Caro enthusiastically though the two were strangers. Her mother had saved Caro a plate from dinner, wrapped in tinfoil in the fridge, and made a big show of re-tossing the salad and reheating the salmon in the oven, as Elsa's father loomed at the division between the kitchen and the tiled entryway. Her mother fussed over Caro, making sure she had everything she needed: water, utensils, a linen napkin, which she picked over the others in the drawer, used already or wrinkled. Elsa watched with a smirk as Caro overperformed her gratitude. Once Caro was settled on her stool, dinner in front of her, Elsa's parents hugged them both and went to bed.

"You're getting the special treatment."

Elsa leaned against the counter opposite Caro's stool.

"Will you sit? You're making me self-conscious," Caro said.

"More water?" Elsa pointed to Caro's empty glass.

Caro nodded and asked if there was any tea.

"Of course."

Elsa turned on the electric kettle and went over to the cabinet to present Caro with the available options.

"Chamomile is fine," Caro said, after thinking it over a minute. Elsa made herself one as well, though it wasn't her habit.

The two remained as they had been, with Caro seated and Elsa standing across from her, each bobbing a teabag thoughtfully.

"So how's it been?" Caro spoke quietly. "Is that a weird thing to ask?"

The absurdity of her predicament dawned on Elsa as she stood in her parents' kitchen, and she saw herself as if from very far away, as if looking back as a much older woman. With Caro suddenly before her, asking innocently enough how it had been, Elsa's guard was let down and the hurt came rushing in. She recalled the man and the woman, that they had been real, and so, too, the loss.

"It's been okay," Elsa said, squeezing the teabag over the mug before placing it in her open palm. Elsa extended her hand out to Caro to indicate that she should discard hers there as well. Caro obeyed and Elsa walked over to toss them both in the compost by the sink, which smelled of rotting fruit. She tried not to gag.

When Caro was finished, Elsa reached for her empty plate, placing it in the sink rather than the dishwasher just beside it.

"Do you want to sit over there?" Elsa asked, her tone still hushed, gesturing to the white, worn couches in the living room beyond.

"Will we wake your parents?" Caro asked.

"Maybe."

Neither moved.

"Maybe we should go upstairs," Elsa offered.

She asked if Caro would like anything else. Caro said that she was fine with what she had—the tea and the water—and Elsa bent to carry Caro's bag, beckoning her friend down the hall toward the back stairs which led up to her bedroom, separate from what she had come to think of as her parents' side of the house.

"You look skinny," Caro whispered, following Elsa up the steps.

"Thanks," Elsa whispered back.

"I didn't mean it as a compliment."

The two reached the landing and continued down the hall in silence. Elsa shut the bedroom door behind her, depositing her friend's belongings gently on the floor by the foot of her childhood bed, and watched as Caro placed both cups on the bedside table before slumping onto the covers in mock exhaustion. Elsa smiled and perched herself toward the foot, so as to maximize the distance. She anticipated a restless night of sleep, by now unaccustomed to the presence of foreign bodies beside her.

"Do you feel like talking about it?" Caro asked, eyes half shut against the low light of the lamp which stood on the bedside table.

Elsa had been circling around the answer to this question since the rupture. She looked down at her hand which lay splayed on the duvet, tracing the veins that rose to support her weight.

"I can't tell if I'm thinking about them all the time, or not at all."

She was uncertain whether the tidying expert and the tingling in her extremities and the fixing around her lungs and the actor-character belonged, at least in part, to the complex network of thoughts and feelings surrounding the man and the woman, or if they had eradicated and supplanted them, becoming objects of rumination in their own right, distinct from and independent of her grief or fear or whatever else lay beneath the numbness.

"Okay, well, I'm here, whatever you need from me right now," Caro said.

Elsa felt the blood in her veins quicken its pumping, accompanied by the urge to ask what Caro thought she could possibly do, given all that had transpired, but she stopped herself from saying so, out of some combination of fatigue and an instinct for self-preservation, one she had not recognized in herself for some time. Caro was the final tether. Elsa had lived with her for several weeks before moving home.

"I don't need anything, really," Elsa replied. "You're the one who wanted to come."

As she said this, Elsa recognized it as an attempt to push the boundary, to figure out where they stood and if it was the same as it had always been. Caro turned to Elsa.

"Maybe it's me who needs you, then."

Elsa wished to turn away, but the self-preservation crept in again, and she found herself crawling instead toward the head of the bed to lay down on the pillow beside Caro.

"Well then," she said, a smile spreading across her face as she looked over at her friend. "What can I do for you?"

Caro repositioned herself so the two lay facing one another in the fetal position, knees and elbows nearly touching. They had lain this way countless times before, their interdependence almost conspiratorial ever since college, as if their friendship were one protracted confession.

"You're impossible."

"Is it okay if we try to get some sleep and catch up tomorrow?" Elsa asked, turning onto her back to stare up at the ceiling.

"Sure," Caro said. She shifted up onto one elbow and looked around the room. "What time is it?"

Elsa reached over to the desk and found her phone. A banner notification sent her heart racing, but it was only a text from her mother, asking her to keep it down. *Daddy and I are sleeping*, she had written, which was a strange way of putting it, as that was clearly not the case. Elsa put her phone face down on the bed between them.

"You're not going to tell me?"

"Oh, sorry," Elsa replied, picking the phone back up.

She tapped its darkened screen so that it lit up, and moved the device up to Caro's face, close enough that it was almost touching her nose, far too close for her to be able to read the time. Caro rolled her eyes and grabbed Elsa's wrist, moving the phone back to a suitable distance.

"Late enough," Caro said, squinting. "Where's the bathroom?"

"Just down the hall," Elsa replied. She watched Caro crouch to the ground and ruffle through her bag, retrieving a small pouch from its depths. Elsa rose from the bed.

"Here, I'll show you," she said.

After Caro returned from the bathroom, Elsa took her place and readied herself for bed, leaving Caro alone. Normally the two would have done so in unison, their conversation continuing even as they brushed their teeth, their words slurred and slow.

Elsa returned to find Caro standing before the open door of her closet.

"What?"

"It's color coded," Caro said.

"So?" Elsa asked, moving to shut the small door.

"It's just kind of—creepy."

"You should see my drawers."

Before she could stop her, Caro walked over to the dresser and opened the second drawer from the top. She glanced at Elsa's neatly folded T-shirts before looking up at her, eyebrows raised.

"Are you, like, okay?"

"Shut up," Elsa said, reopening the door to her closet. She grabbed the first shirt she could find off a hanger and threw it at Caro. It was a near miss. The shirt fluttered down to the floor beside Caro's feet.

That night, Elsa lay still, feeling the weight of her friend sleeping beside her. She imagined Caro's body as that of the actor-character, resisting the impulse to reach out and stroke her hair. In the dark, Elsa followed Caro's steady breath in the silence which had descended between them, like love.

Elsa woke to find Caro seated upright beside her in bed, reading a paperback. She felt a heaviness in her limbs and suspected she had slept poorly, her body holding the memory of fitful agitation.

"Morning, sunshine," Caro said, smiling. The sarcasm in her voice undermined the corniness of the phrase.

Elsa reached up to place her hand on her friend's face, palming it gently like a basketball. She felt Caro's eyelashes flutter against her skin.

"What are you doing?" Caro asked, her voice muffled. Though she could not see her mouth, Elsa could feel her friend smiling.

"Just making sure you're real," Elsa replied.

The two drove into town and sat at a shady table outside the coffee shop. Elsa looked around with anticipation, but it was early. The lawn was empty, apart from a group of six men who appeared all over seventy, wearing variations of the same uniform: slacks despite the heat, polo shirts, and baseball caps in the colors of the college. The actor-character was probably sleeping.

"It's so quaint," Caro had said on their way in, taking in the rolling pastures from the driver's seat. She had her own car, and so Elsa let her drive, happy to drift along in the passenger seat. She remembered that she had not replied to her mother's text from the night before.

"Is there anything you want to see while you're here?" Elsa asked, stabbing at the ice in her coffee with a plastic straw.

"You, mainly," Caro said. She sat with her legs bent, shins pushed up against the edge of the table.

"Besides that."

"I was hoping you'd tell me," Caro responded. "What is there to do here? Or, what have you been doing?"

They were two different questions, and Elsa said so. Once again, she felt as if Caro's visit was an accusation, or worse, a checkup.

"I'm recovering," Elsa said after a moment, ironically. The answer seemed to satisfy, and Caro's response was sincere, matter-of-fact.

"Fair enough."

"What about you?" Elsa asked.

"What about me?"

"I don't know. What's up?"

They both laughed. Caro told her that things were good, mostly. That her dissertation was going fine, that the city was unbearably hot. "The heat makes me stupid," Caro said, and Elsa wondered silently if that was perhaps her problem as well. "I can't get any thinking done."

"How's Liv?" Elsa asked. She had still not met Caro's girlfriend, but she felt skeptical, protective as she always did, unable to mirror Caro's incessant graciousness when it came to the men—always men, until the man and the woman—Elsa had chosen to love.

"She's good. She's on a deadline right now, so she's going a little crazy and I don't get to see her much. But we're thinking of moving in together, which might fix some of that." Caro had been making easy eye contact the whole time, but looked away as she uttered the final sentence.

"That's fast."

"It's been eight months, actually." Caro was now looking straight at her. "And you're one to talk."

It was true that though Elsa had only left the city two months ago, she had been absent in many ways long before that. It had been Caro's couch she'd slept on after the breakup, when she still had hopes of finding another place in the city; Caro was the one to pick her up off the floor, metaphorically but also—once—literally, in the aftermath. In the weeks Elsa stayed with Caro, Liv had never once come around. It occurred to Elsa only now that Caro had been protecting the delicate thing that had sprung between herself and Liv by not introducing them. Liv, the butch sculptor with all the tattoos whom Elsa had yet to meet.

"Who's she showing with?"

"Don't worry," Caro said, intuiting what was unspoken. "It's with some blue-chip gallery in Chelsea. Which is why she's pulling all-nighters at the studio. This show could make her career."

When Elsa said nothing, Caro added, "It's not with them."

Though the referent pronoun was vague, there was no question to whom it pertained. Elsa thought of the man and the woman and the gallery downtown and the industrial space which held all the man's pieces in Greenpoint. She looked around, but the actor-character was nowhere in sight.

"Okay," Elsa said in response.

"What else should we do?"

"You've pretty much seen it all," Elsa said, gesturing grandly up and down the one-way street.

"It's so green," Caro continued. "Everything smells different in the country. Like fresh-mown grass and gravel and dew."

"You should consider moving. We could start a commune. Liv could come too. You know I'm all about communal living," Elsa replied.

Caro looked at Elsa to see if she was joking.

"Don't threaten me with a good time."

Neither of them spoke for a long while.

"Can we go for a walk after this?" Caro asked.

"Do you want to take a stroll up the street? See all the wonderful shops my hometown has to offer?" Elsa asked.

"No. Like a walk in nature."

"The city girl wants a nature walk," Elsa said.

"Absolutely, I do."

"Well then, that's what she'll get."

Elsa instructed Caro to park the car at her parents' house and led her friend on foot toward the hill in the opposite direction from the road leading into town. The few neighboring homes dissipated into farmland on the right and the land conservation on the left, and cows grazed lazily in the afternoon heat, which was mild—Caro reminded Elsa, who had been complaining—compared to the city.

"Have you thought about what you'll do?" Caro asked. The two had been trudging silently up the steep, dirt road.

Elsa kicked a stone ahead of her.

"What do you mean?" She kept her gaze on the stone and, when she came upon it, kicked it further up the hill.

"I mean here. Or from here."

Elsa stopped and stared out at the landscape.

"I haven't."

Caro stopped too, a few steps ahead, and turned back to face her. Elsa could feel her friend's eyes on her, but she kept her attention directed toward the pastures, deep green from days of rain followed by sun, and watched the cows graze with envy. Perhaps, in spite of the impulses that led her to the man and the woman, she had always longed for simplicity. But she could not see through the thickness of her days, could not find a path either back to where she had been, or forward to some unknown point.

"Are you worried about money?" Caro asked.

"I got a job at a restaurant," she replied.

"So you're planning on staying?"

"I don't know," Elsa said. "For now."

"Were you able to save anything in all that time?" Caro asked. "Like, could you move back and find a job once you're settled?"

It was the third time Caro had alluded to the man and the woman, even if it was her manner to speak around it, and Elsa said nothing. She wished instead to confess to the tingling in her extremities and the fixing around her lungs and the blood in her veins and clocks ticking, but her resistance was twofold: she doubted her ability to articulate these feelings and she feared that, through articulation, such preoccupations would become material. Her refusal to profess these sensations allowed her to preserve a kind of future deniability, which she hoped might leave her in eventual doubt of their ever having occurred at all.

"I texted her," Elsa said instead.

She began to walk, and Caro followed.

"Why?"

"Because I was running a little low on self-loathing. I needed a top-up."

"Elsa—" Caro said gravely, but nothing more.

The two had reached the crest of the steepest part of the hill, and the road continued on at an incline, but a flattish one, more manageable. They continued walking in silence, up toward where the land grew flat and a small pond spilled out from a tunnel beneath the road on both sides, where beavers had built an intricate web of dams. As a child, Elsa had walked there with her parents on summer evenings, the three of them waiting in silent anticipation for the surfacing of a small, brown head, or a wide, flat tail, which floated, like a log, along the top of the water.

"Did she respond?"

The two had stopped walking and stood by the edge of the pond. Elsa leaned against the metal guardrail and watched as a pair of geese flew down to land on the water.

"Of course not," Elsa replied.

"Good," Caro said simply.

Elsa looked at her friend to see if she was aware of her cruelty.

"Fuck her," Caro added, with more affect than she had displayed all weekend. And then, after a thoughtful moment, "And fuck him, too."

That evening Caro drove Elsa into town for ice cream. They were full from dinner with Elsa's parents, but it was early and they were both restless. The two sat in silence, neither one attentive to the radio playing softly from the car's speakers, as Caro regarded the dusk beyond the windshield. They parked in Elsa's usual spot. Voices rose and fell as they crossed the lot in the direction of a small wooden structure which stood on risers in the middle of a lawn, opposite the coffee shop where they had sat earlier that day. A line of families and couples snaked its way from the grass up the steps, and as they approached the small building, Elsa spotted a circle of bodies draped over Adirondack chairs out front. Though it is possible she retroactively instilled the memory with a strange, predictive sensation, Elsa would later recall a somatic awareness of the actor-character's proximity as they neared the ice cream shop before she was able to confirm by sight, seconds later, that it was indeed him, seated nonchalantly, surrounded by a small group, an empty paper cup discarded at his feet.

Caro reached out a hand and gripped Elsa's forearm. "Is that—"

A rush of blood, a reddening of the face; Elsa removed her arm from Caro's grasp.

"Do you know who that is?" Caro whispered, too loudly for Elsa's comfort as they joined the back of the line.

The couple in front of them turned back to look at Caro and Elsa before scanning the scattered bodies on the grass. The group continued their animated chat, oblivious or perhaps long-immune to onlookers. Elsa ignored Caro.

"What's he doing here?"

"He's in a play," Elsa finally replied, her voice low. She squinted meaningfully at her friend as the woman in the couple turned around again.

"What?" Caro asked, once the woman had turned to face the front, refusing to lower her voice. The line took a collective step forward and Caro craned her neck in the direction of the group. "Who's that with him?"

"Who?"

By now the group was behind them and Elsa resisted the urge to turn around.

"The dyke. The hot one. Or at least I think it's a dyke." Caro squinted at the group.

"Or a very pretty boy."

Without looking, Elsa knew Caro was referring to the person whom she had seen on her first sighting of the actor-character, the one who had pet Sasha and nodded to her as they passed one another on the street.

"How would I know?" Elsa replied.

"They're wearing a beaded necklace," Caro muttered. "Tricky, tricky."

As the two approached the window, Elsa envisioned herself being watched by the actor-character and the person beside him. A teenage girl leaned out to greet them.

"What can I get you?" she asked.

Caro studied the flavors on the chalkboard.

"Can I get a scoop of cookie dough?"

"Cup or cone?"

"Cone, please," Caro replied.

The teenage girl disappeared from the window, returning moments later with the ice cream. Caro thanked her, licking the side where a clump had broken free, and turned to Elsa.

"What do you want? I'm buying." The words came out muffled, the side of her mouth still attached to the cone.

"I'll have the same," Elsa replied.

Once they had paid and moved down the steps to the side of the building, Elsa was unsure where to turn her attention. The actor-character was a forcefield which both attracted and repelled—she could attend to nothing else, yet something stopped her from looking directly.

"Let's sit," she heard herself say.

Caro led the way to a pair of empty chairs further down the lawn and Elsa followed, noting the presence of the person next to the actor-character. She sensed their gaze follow her as she passed, though she was too shy to check. Glancing over her shoulder before taking her seat next to Caro, Elsa caught the person's eye. Had they nodded in her direction, or had she imagined it in the dusk which had settled around them?

Elsa shifted purposefully to face away from the group, focusing instead on Caro, though she felt the cells of her back rising, receptive to whatever stimuli drifted her way from the actor-character's orbit. It occurred to her that ears were not the only organs for listening, that one could also hear with the blade of a shoulder, the kidneys, the heart, the skin.

"If you had to fuck one person from that group, who would it be?" Caro asked. She was leaned back, her legs draped over the flat, unvarnished arm of the Adirondack chair.

Elsa nearly feigned ignorance as to which group Caro was referring, but that would only push her friend further. Caro looked over to the bodies surrounding the actor-character and then back to Elsa.

"I'd fuck him. But only once. For the story."

Elsa looked over at him. He wore a white T-shirt under a denim sleeveless jacket, a white baseball cap.

"I thought you swore off men in college."

"Eh," Caro said with a shrug. "What even is gender anymore? Now you go."

"I don't know," Elsa said, looking from the actor-character to the person seated beside him.

"Oh, please. You'd obviously fuck him."

"Why do you say that?"

"Because he's gorgeous and, like, incredibly famous. Who else are you going to fuck in that group? Those gay men? The dyke?"

"If you're so certain, then why are you asking?" Elsa asked, not sure why she was refusing to agree. "It feels loaded."

"Loaded how?"

"Like it's a veiled question about my sexuality."

"It's just a hypothetical question. I'm trying to get a sense of your type these days. Which is—?"

"I don't know."

"Men."

"Not necessarily," Elsa said.

"I've never been informed otherwise," Caro said, licking the exterior of her cone.

The two stared at one another in silence.

"That's not true," Elsa said, finally.

Caro paused for a moment. "Dating a couple doesn't make you gay."

"I've never claimed it did," Elsa said, her voice betraying a defensiveness that surprised her.

She heard the voice of the actor-character rise above the hum and felt its vibrational frequency somewhere near her rib cage.

"Are you interested in dating women?" Caro asked.

"I don't know."

"Okay, so—"

"But it's not like I haven't fucked, or, like, slept with a woman."

"I'm not sure that counts."

"Why not?" Elsa asked.

"Because there was always a dick in the room."

Elsa was unable to tune out the sounds of the group and felt herself split in two. Laughter broke out, but the actor-character's was the loudest; she felt it move inside her, unable to locate the seam along which he ended and she began. From two separate but simultaneous points, she began to laugh, which caused the laughter to redouble and rise in pitch.

Elsa pictured a game from her childhood: bodies laid in a zig-zag formation, each head resting on a neighbor's stomach. Feigned laughter turned real. She pictured her selves multiplying into an endless chain. *Ha ha*, her selves said, one after another, a multiplicity devolving into hysterics. And so she laughed, unable to stop herself, though the actor-character had long ceased, as had Caro. She failed to notice both.

Elsa wiped away tears and detected in Caro's face a kind of suspension, as if awaiting a cue before deciding where to land. This look returned her to herself, and she was able to stop, feeling suddenly somber. Her laughter moments prior echoed in the ensuing silence and made her self-conscious. The group behind her had grown quiet.

"What?" she asked, bringing a finger to dab one eye, then the other.

"I missed something," Caro said.

"What do you mean?"

Elsa turned to find the group had disbanded. She watched the actor-character's tall frame retreat toward the parking lot.

"Why were you laughing like that?" Caro asked, turning to follow her gaze and then back to Elsa.

"Because it's not true," she said, returning to face Caro.

"What isn't?"

"That there was a dick in the room. Not always. And you know that," Elsa replied.

"Well, if not literally, then metaphorically."

"So you're saying there's no dick, literal or metaphorical, in the room with you and Liv?"

"Ha!" Caro let out a loud laugh. "Wow. Fair enough."

Elsa finished her ice cream, wishing she had brought her pack of cigarettes. Caro looked over her shoulder at the few remaining silhouettes of the group.

"That person keeps looking at you."

"**D**o you want a cigarette?" Elsa asked.

It was 11:38 a.m.

"Since when did you start smoking again?"

The two were sitting across from one another on the patio facing the garden. Elsa ignored the question and instead replied as she rose from her seat, feeling the rush of caffeine on an empty stomach, "Come."

Caro followed, pausing to grab the two empty mugs Elsa had intended to leave on the table.

"Thanks. You can just leave them in the sink," Elsa said when they entered the kitchen from the back door.

Caro ignored Elsa and rinsed both cups before bending to place them in the dishwasher.

"Saint Caro," Elsa said as she turned to wait in the threshold between the kitchen and the front entrance. It had been intended as a compliment, but she watched Caro's face darken.

The two made their way up the stairs in silence and into Elsa's room, where she reached for the pack on the dresser and walked over to the window by the desk. "Come," she said again, looking back at her friend and climbing through.

"Is it safe?" Caro asked. She put a tentative knee on the desk, but her other foot remained squarely on the floor.

"Of course."

Elsa sat on the roof, legs bent toward the hazy sky. She listened to

Caro scramble through the window and turned to watch her settle beside her, noting her friend's beauty, which was especially evident in this moment, with the soft light from behind outlining her head like a halo. Sensing Caro's distraction, Elsa took the occasion to linger, as Caro reached to tuck the fine strands of hair which had fallen into her face behind a delicate, almost translucent ear.

"What?" Caro asked, suddenly feeling herself watched.

Elsa ignored the inquiry and withdrew two cigarettes from the pack, which had become soft and worn at its seams, handing one to Caro.

"Here."

She lit Caro's cigarette first, who bent to meet the flame, her hair falling loose and into her face. Elsa studied the graceful hand that shot up instinctively to tuck the hairs back in place once more. Caro lifted her head, blowing a long exhale of smoke.

The two sat in what would have been silence but for the birds and the lawn mower down the road and the distant traffic. Both looked out at the green beneath them, hands moving in slow intervals between mouths and knees.

"I don't know how to reach you." Caro stared at the trees beyond.

"This seems really naïve in retrospect," she continued when Elsa failed to respond, "but I thought me just being here would be of help in some way. I thought you were unreachable because of the literal distance between us. That if I could gain some proximity—" She trailed off. Her cigarette had burned halfway down.

Elsa felt the words float between them and tried to gain hold so that she might respond. She became overwhelmed by the sensation that she and Caro were both actors in a movie, bound to some script whose lines she continually failed to remember. She pondered what the actor-character would do in such a situation, and thought of his attentive presence in all the various moments of his life as the inverse of her own absence, like two opposing poles. Elsa felt her hand reach for Caro's thigh. As if at a distance, she watched herself move in closer. She felt Caro grow rigid, but not before her lips made contact, briefly, with the fullness of her friend's half-open mouth. The body beside her—a body Elsa had disembodied, for it was not Caro, nor any body in particular she sought—jerked suddenly in retreat.

"What the fuck!" Caro exclaimed, her voice shaking with the force of containing what Elsa determined was, with equal likelihood, either rage or laughter.

Elsa looked at her friend in stunned silence and burst into tears. Her sobbing cut through the hardness in her chest, and for the first time since she had moved home, a vast space unfurled inside her. She wanted to swim around in it, the space of her sobbing, with Caro unmoving beside her; she could not stop herself, nor did she wish to, feeling herself overcome by a dizzying mix of dread and optimism.

Dreadful optimism, optimistic dread, she thought to herself, and as she did, just as suddenly as the tears and the hole and the hope had opened up, Elsa constricted. Her tears dried up, and she became aware once more of the fixing on her lungs and the pumping of her blood and the shelf in her heart, along with a new sensation: Caro's hand on the small of her back. Elsa could not determine the contours of Caro's feeling.

"I'm sorry," Elsa said, wiping the tears off her cheek.

"It's fine," Caro said.

"It's honestly fine," she said again, this time with more conviction. After a moment, Caro continued. "Just promise me you'll never do that again."

She stubbed her cigarette and flicked the butt into the grass below before Elsa could stop her.

"I promise," Elsa said. "I'm not in love with you or anything. I don't know why I did that."

"Okay. Well, that's good."

Elsa watched Caro trace her finger in circles over the wooden slats as she looked out toward the road beyond the trees.

"I also just think you might be—" Caro paused in search of the right wording.

"Bi?" Elsa asked.

"I was going to say depressed."

They looked at each other and burst into laughter. Elsa noted within herself a desire to move once more through the space of her weeping, but the moment had passed, and she knew no more tears would come.

—

Do you want to talk about what happened this weekend? Elsa read the text from Caro but did not respond.

———

I don't feel like I need to, unless you do, Elsa wrote back two days later.

———

I'd like to talk about it at some point. But it doesn't have to be right now. Let me know whenever you are ready. Elsa wondered at the word "ready," and whether or not she had ever felt it.

E lsa sat opposite the therapist.

"How are you?" she asked.

"I'm fine," the therapist replied. "How are you?"

It was a script, by now familiar, in which the two indulged. She considered the question and for a moment recalled the soft downward pull of grief after kissing Caro. She wondered if she could conjure the feeling now, but as she groped, she encountered instead the force of her own resistance. It occurred to her that she might confess all of this—the kiss, perhaps, but also the particular potency of her numbness—to the therapist opposite her, who was waiting in patient silence.

And so she did. Or at the very least tried to, faltering when she failed to locate the correct word. She redacted and revised, introducing parentheticals that were meant to clarify but which she feared only increased the unintelligibility of the smattering of physical sensations that she wished to communicate. As if caught in an undertow, the more words she expounded to make herself known, the farther she found herself from the shore of comprehension.

"Have you ever tried just sitting with it?" the woman asked, finding entry through a pause in Elsa's monologue.

"With what?"

"The numbness. The resistance, or whatever you want to call it."

When Elsa did not speak, the woman continued. "Rather than rushing to find out what's beneath it or willing the sensations away, would it be possible to sit still and breathe into them wherever they arise—in your hands, in your chest, in your feet?"

"Like meditation?"

"You can call it whatever you want. If meditation is appealing to you, then it could be something to look into. I'll leave that up to you. But what I detect in everything you just told me is an immense amount of struggle. And I wonder if it might be possible for you to approach the resistance with a little more ease, even a little—" The woman paused. "Compassion."

As she concluded her thought, Elsa detected the final word inscribe its meaning on the therapist's face as a gentle crinkling of the skin around the outer corners of her eyes, a hairline fracture in her porcelain features. Though Elsa could have been overreading, she experienced the phenomenon as a minor rebellion of emotion against the therapist's cosmetic incapacity to emote.

Elsa stood at the desk inside the lobby. She was alone this evening, having completed her training. When guests arrived, she reminded herself to smile as she greeted them and led them to their tables. She wished guests a good meal and remembered, though not always, to remove excess settings. On her way back to the host stand, she alerted the servers to new arrivals in their sections.

On slower nights she was allowed to read a book, but she never remembered to bring one. Instead, she spent her free time searching the internet, though where she had been or what she had learned by the end of her shift she could not recall. Drawn to the website of a particular social media platform, she discovered that the restaurant's account remained logged in—allowing her to search for the woman nightly, unblocked, to see if any changes in her life had occurred, or at least the parts of her life as she chose to display them publicly, though not a public that included Elsa.

On busier evenings, she had little time to read the internet or search for clues of the man or the woman, and instead spent her shift apologizing for things over which she had little to no control: the restaurant's inadequate space for parking; the slowness of diners to depart tables promised to other guests, who were now standing in front of Elsa, demanding to be seated; the inexplicable lack of cellular service on the particular stretch of road on which the restaurant was located; the lengthiness of the Wi-Fi password, inevitably requested by guests unable to receive or send texts, and which Elsa distributed each evening, writing the random sequence of letters and numbers by hand on scraps of paper, copied from a printed version taped to the filing cabinet beneath the desk, hidden from view to anyone but Elsa. When things got truly out of hand and the lobby became full of bodies, some spilling out onto the porch by the door, her manager would move behind the desk beside Elsa to temper the onslaught, allowing Elsa to slip out and around the corner with the iPad in hand to survey the dining room for soon-to-be-open tables, sometimes—too often for her liking—clearing and resetting them herself, whenever the bussers were nowhere to be found.

She was free to leave every evening at ten when the kitchen closed. Though she was allowed a drink, she never took one. Each night at the close of her shift she stood at the threshold of the dining room and waited to be released.

E lsa turned to the door of the restaurant in greeting, though it had only been the wind. She thought of her health care, which she had applied for through the state, and of her discovery, and the subsequent mix of shame and relief, that her hostess salary put her technically below the poverty line and therefore granted her fully subsidized coverage. Two guests entered the lobby from the dining room, and Elsa smiled as they thanked her for the lovely dinner, waving goodbye from the door.

The couple stepped aside to let someone enter. It was the person whom Elsa had twice seen with the actor-character. They advanced toward her and asked if the kitchen was still open, and, if so, were there two seats available at the bar. Elsa noted a solitary thin gold hoop that hugged the lobe of their left ear and felt a tingling in her hands and face as she reached out to check the time, tapping the iPad in front of her. It was 9:56 p.m., a Friday.

"The kitchen technically closes in just a few minutes, but it should be fine. Do you mind waiting here while I check with my manager?"

As Elsa was rounding the desk, a woman entered and greeted the person with a kiss.

"What's the verdict?" the woman asked, pulling away.

The friend of the actor-character rested a hand gently on their date's lower back and nodded toward Elsa.

"We're about to find out."

As they spoke, they smiled at Elsa in a way she struggled to define. Was it faintly teasing, or, Elsa wondered, noting a resurgence of a tingling in her extremities, perhaps flirtatious? She was unsure whether or not they recognized her.

"Great," the date said.

Finding her cue, Elsa resumed her trajectory and entered the back of the kitchen. A server was on his phone, leaning against the counter beside a rack of unpolished glassware.

"Have you seen Alex?"

He gave a jerk of his head, not bothering to look up from his device, to indicate that Elsa should go through the opposite doors and onto the floor of the restaurant.

When Elsa reached the end of the bar where her manager stood chatting with the sole bartender that evening and asked if she could seat two latecomers, the manager looked at her watch before replying, "We're technically still open. Sorry," she sighed, turning to the bartender.

"Great," Elsa said. "Or, I mean, sorry, yeah—" and turned on her heels back the way she had come.

As Elsa entered the lobby once more, she heard hushed voices which stopped short as soon as the couple became aware of her presence.

"So?" the date asked. The two stood somewhat further apart than when Elsa had left them, no longer touching.

"Right this way," Elsa said, and began to walk them through the short hallway and onto the floor of the restaurant, stopping once the bar was clearly in sight to indicate, with an outstretched arm and an open hand, the bar's general direction. Max had scolded her on one of her first nights for pointing with her finger.

"Have a seat anywhere you like."

Back behind the front desk, Elsa noted a desire to return to her online searches, but the energy of the evening had shifted and eliminated her sense of privacy. Though she refused to confront the belief head-on, there persisted an underlying impression that the person at the bar might somehow be able to intuit her thoughts, and her usual objects of ruminative fantasy became laced with danger: the actor-character was off-limits, as was the subject of the man and the woman, as were the pair themselves—a novel interest—now seated at the bar.

The train of thought was interrupted by the sound of footsteps in the hall as the person emerged into the lobby and stood before her, head bent toward their phone.

"I was told they ran out of slips for the password at the bar and no one seems to know it offhand. Can you tell me the Wi-Fi password?"

"Oh, yeah," Elsa said. "That's because it's, like, really long."

They smiled at her. At their lopsided grin, Elsa noted a tingling in her hands which made its way through her body and into her pelvis, a new sensation.

"Let me write it down for you," she said.

They did not respond, watching silently as Elsa took a piece of scrap paper and, having to bend slightly to read the code taped to the filing cabinet beneath the desk, began to diligently copy the password in a semi-crouched position. She could not help but feel that there was something sexual, something dominant in the way the person stood in silence, contemplating Elsa as she bent before them in servitude. When Elsa rose to hand over the slip of paper, they held the same beguiling smile. It was only then that Elsa noted their dimples. She guessed from the slight furrows of their brow and the hint of lines forming around their eyes and mouth that they must be in their late thirties, despite their boyish looks. Their dark brown hair was parted down the middle, just long enough to be tucked behind each ear. The piece of paper passed through hands which did not touch.

"Thanks."

By now Elsa had grown to anticipate the heat of her face, which only sealed her blushing's eventual occurrence.

"I think I've seen you around town," they said.

"Yeah," Elsa replied. "You may have pet my dog once?"

She regretted the way her statement had risen in pitch, coming out as a question in need of confirmation, rather than allowing it to float between them as possibility.

"Huh," they said. "What kind of dog?"

"Golden retriever."

"Fancy."

Elsa laughed. "She belongs to my parents."

"Well, the three of us will have to meet again so you can reintroduce us. Officially."

"Right," Elsa said, letting out a strange laugh.

"I'm Sam, by the way."

They did not extend their hand, so Elsa did not shake it. Instead, they both maintained their positions as mirror images of one another, hands resting on their respective sides of the desk.

"Elsa."

"I should probably get back to my girlfriend."

The person called Sam wore the same smile which Elsa could not read. They did not await a reply and walked back into the dining room, leaving Elsa alone.

Elsa lay in bed and studied the grooved shapes on the wooden ceiling above her. Her fingers moved periodically, as if of their own accord, to trace the outline of her underwear. Each time Elsa became aware of their trajectory, she moved her hand once more to rest on the mattress beside her, afraid of what sorts of pleasures she might envision. The person called Sam had made their way to the forefront of Elsa's thoughts, and she resisted the urge to reach for her phone, knowing the sorts of yearnings it activated.

Her curiosity about the person called Sam was twofold: their presence during Elsa's first encounter with the actor-character caused them to be permanently associated with him, functioning as a conduit of sorts. But Elsa also intuited an underbelly to her curiosity about them: something physical and uncalculated, the jerk of a knee, a string that tugged. And it was this element that perplexed and frightened her and kept her from touching herself and carrying the fantasy through. This thought, which was not quite a thought—Elsa did not allow herself to fully think it—nagged as she sat up and looked around the room. She reached for her phone. It was eleven in the morning.

She stood and made her way over to the windows and raised the blinds. Her eyes adjusted to the light and she made out the pack of cigarettes—she had replaced the first pack with a second, and then a third—which lay on her dresser. She grabbed it, along with her lighter, and climbed out onto the roof outside her bedroom window.

Once she had settled herself and lit her cigarette, she inhaled deeply, smoke filling her lungs. It unnerved her, this pull toward the person called Sam. She was further unnerved by the fact that the person called Sam appeared to apprehend something about Elsa, of which she herself was mostly unaware—a kind of inclination which she had not yet confirmed.

But perhaps she was reading too much into that aspect, the flirtation, the sexual charge of the night before, the troubling and unnecessary referencing of the girlfriend waiting alone at the bar. Elsa noted the resurfacing of a feeling which she had not felt since before the rupture with the man and the woman and which therefore disconcerted her, having believed she had rid herself of the impulse.

She wished to contact Caro, which is to say she wished to confide.

Instead, Elsa stubbed out her cigarette and stood, dizzy from the combination of tobacco on an empty stomach and the heat of the morning, to duck inside her room.

———

On her computer's browser, Elsa searched "Sam" and the name of her hometown.

———

Elsa searched "Sam" and the name of the theater festival.

———

Elsa searched "Sam" and the name of the actor-character. She found nothing.

———

Elsa made herself a coffee with cream in the empty kitchen and did not drive into town.

When Elsa arrived at the coffee shop—the primary site of encounter—she stood in line and looked around in a way she hoped would appear casual, willing herself to believe that it was for the presence of the actor-character that she scanned the sparsely seated room. The girl behind the register was the same one who had fetched the manager for her interview. She smiled shyly at Elsa, who attempted to return the greeting as she ordered her usual drink. She wondered if the girl remembered her, or if her friendliness was more general. The girl spoke tentatively.

"Hey, did you ever end up finding a job?"

"Oh, um, yeah, kind of."

"Cool," the girl said, her gaze not quite meeting Elsa's.

The girl deposited the change into Elsa's open palm and Elsa tipped its contents—more than twice as much as the drink itself had cost—into the jar before her. She regretted the action before its completion but could think of no way to gracefully abort the gesture. As her fingers parted with the worn bills, Elsa felt sick over the loss, noting that there was once a time when she wouldn't have thought twice about parting with such a sum.

"Oh wow, thank you." The girl's eyes widened in surprise.

"You're welcome," Elsa mumbled over her shoulder, walking toward the other end of the counter to await her drink.

She felt the presence of a body beside her and turned to find the person called Sam. The two looked at one another and Elsa was about to say hello, when someone called their name.

They both turned to find the actor-character standing behind them, and Elsa stepped aside as the two hugged. When the barista called her name, it took a moment for Elsa to recognize it as her own. She moved to place a lid on her drink and headed toward the door. As her hand made contact with the metal handle, she turned back once more toward the pair. The actor-character was facing away from her, but the person called Sam issued a nod in her direction.

The rest of the day, Elsa lay in bed and watched her thoughts as they shifted from the man and the woman to the actor-character, and, more frequently than she would have liked, to the person called Sam. And though she had not planned the encounter, per se, she nevertheless felt a sense of having been caught red-handed. As in times before, Elsa felt herself drawn to this sort of slippage, a loosening of the grip on the reins of her life, and she would give herself over to the will and fates of others. She would float, she thought, picturing the bed on which she now lay as a boat in water, wherever the tides took her. She began to feel the descension of a headache.

That evening, the ibuprofen having delivered its relief, Elsa fell asleep to half-formed images of the actor-character and the person called Sam, whom she pictured sitting on either side of her reclined body, stroking her head before suddenly growing cross, varyingly uttering words of praise, then reproach, then praise once more. She felt herself argue, protest, but whenever she stepped back from the brink of sleep in an effort to reconstruct the confused dialogues which she had conjured, she was unable to follow their logic. When she woke in the morning, she possessed only a dim recollection of the confused discourse from the previous night.

The theater season picked up and Elsa had less time to ruminate, the moments behind the front desk diminishing at a steady rate until she barely had time to seat one party before the next arrived. The servers no longer wandered by for idle chat and merely acknowledged her presence with a hurried nod whenever they passed one another on the floor or in the small passageway between the lobby and the dining room. On good nights, Elsa welcomed the predictability of her motions—greet, seat, circle through the kitchen and back to the desk—her body in flow, the harried importance of the servers a kind of contagion, as she noted within herself an inflation of purpose, of becoming a part of a system larger than herself.

In her down moments, Elsa was back on the internet, her fingers searching, even before her desire made itself known, for the person called Sam, or the actor-character, or the man and the woman. It was on a night such as this—hands poised above her keyboard as she toggled between the social profiles of those she both knew and didn't—that she looked up to find the actor-character standing before her.

"Hi," he said brightly.

He took a step closer, and Elsa stood up from the stool where she sat. The actor-character rested his hands on the desk, and Elsa noted the thick silver ring which he wore around his pointer finger.

"Hi," Elsa replied, her habitual script failing her.

The actor-character asked if they had room for five. As he spoke,

Elsa watched the band glint in the light of the candle. His fingers tapped out a tune on the desk, and she thought of how she had circled the town in search of him. Or if not him, then the feeling he had evoked in her. He stood alone, a fact which filled Elsa with hope.

The restaurant's book was heavy that evening, but without first checking the tablet before her, she found herself nodding and leading him silently into the dining room. She willed her hands not to tremble.

"Busy night?" he asked.

"Kind of," Elsa said, adding after a moment, "but that's all right."

She led him to a corner table, laying the menus at each empty seat. The actor-character sat before she was finished, choosing the chair facing the windows, so that his back was turned to the interior of the restaurant. When she asked what name the rest of his party might ask for when they arrived, she felt the same flash of violence which ran through her when she had turned away from him in feigned indifference on the street. When he said simply and without hesitation the name her fingers had sought over and over on keyboards and on the small screen of her phone, she was surprised to find that he used his own; she could not have said what other name she expected.

When the person called Sam arrived with their girlfriend and two others Elsa recognized by sight if not name, she led them directly to the actor-character's table without awaiting confirmation. Their voices echoed as she stood alone in the lobby. Reaching for her phone, she felt the steadiness of a hand no longer trembling.

At the end of her shift, the actor-character's table—which Elsa had come to think of as the table belonging to the person called Sam—was the sole remaining party. Elsa approached the bar through the kitchen, where the three closing servers stood.

"Does someone finally want a shift drink?" the bartender asked.

Elsa spotted a tattoo on the woman's forearm which she had never noticed before.

"Yeah. I think I'll have a glass of wine."

The bartender smiled.

"Which one?"

"A red."

"Give her the Baga," a server said. "It's good, you'll like it," he continued without looking up at her. His head was bent toward his phone, held discreetly beneath the bar.

"Thanks," Elsa replied.

The bartender gave her a heavier pour than she wished to drink, and Elsa stood somewhat apart from the other servers who seemed not to notice her, floating between the bar and the service station toward the kitchen. When she heard the actor-character's name in hushed tones, she moved a step closer.

"You can sit if you want," the bartender said, gesturing toward the empty stools.

Elsa sat and took a sip of wine. It was light and dry, almost effervescent, and she found she did like it. She took another sip, her eyes traveling above the array of bottles, lit from below, and up to the dark windows which lined the restaurant all the way to the back of the bar, reflecting the room's large interior. Hers was a dark outline, the details of her face murky.

"Do you know who that is?" the bartender said to her, interrupting Elsa's thoughts with the tilt of her head in the direction of the actor-character.

Elsa fought the urge to turn in the table's direction.

"He's famous, right?"

"Yeah. He was in that movie."

"Right," Elsa said, feigning sudden recognition. After a pause, she brought the glass to her lips in an effort at nonchalance. "Do you know who else he's with?"

One of the younger female servers who had exchanged almost no words with Elsa moved toward the bar and addressed her.

"That's Sarah Lloyd. She's been in a bunch of movies. And I'm pretty sure the dark-haired woman—or, person, I guess—is her partner. I think they direct or produce or something. I follow Sarah on Instagram."

Elsa looked briefly over her shoulder, taking in the girlfriend of the person called Sam with new interest.

"Is she also in a play here?" Elsa asked, turning back to them.

"Which one? Sarah or her partner?" the server asked.

"Um, Sarah, I guess," Elsa said, the intimacy of the name strange in her mouth.

"Yeah, she is. They're still in rehearsals. I've seen them in here together a few times."

"That's the first time he's come in, though," the bartender said, once again tilting her head to indicate she had meant the actor-character.

"Cool" was all Elsa could think to say.

E lsa sat on the roof and lit a cigarette, reaching for the phone beside her. Moments earlier, she had typed in the name of the girlfriend into one of her social media apps. The bright screen of the device had almost entirely obscured the shapes in the yard beyond, flattening the various shadows into a uniform field of darkness. Elsa felt her world tilt slightly, unsure whether it had to do with the nicotine entering her system or the picturing of an infinite nothingness which extended beyond her tiny phone. Feeling briefly high, she began to scroll through Sarah Lloyd's pictures.

Without having been able to articulate it beforehand, she realized she had expected something edgier, perhaps more aloof, an inaccessibility onto which Elsa could project. Sarah Lloyd was just a woman, it occurred to her, though prettier than most. She scrolled through a series of images from what appeared to be magazine shoots, punctuated by wide shots of what were, Elsa determined from the captions, various stage rehearsals for former plays and stills from movies. In the midst of all this were images, taken by Sarah presumably, of food and latte art. Elsa scrolled through the text below each image, noting the proliferation of emojis and exclamation marks, and felt her interest retreat further. She stubbed out her cigarette and was about to put her phone down when she reached a picture—a selfie—of Sarah smiling, her head tilted so that it touched the bare shoulder of a person sitting beside her. It was Sam. She clicked on the photo to see if they had been tagged.

Her heart beat into the night, though she did not note it, as she clicked over to their profile.

With one hand, she scrolled through photos of paper coasters with torn edges, zoomed-in billboards, pieces of trash scattered on the street. She took a drag and paused on an image: a deteriorating sign which read, "Just a Tease: A Family Hair Salon." Elsa exhaled a sharp laugh, and looked around, though she could not make out her surroundings beyond the roof, whose wooden slats were lit by the light from her room. Elsa scrolled further, slowly this time, and clicked to enlarge a picture. The screen of a cash register displayed the phrase, "Tender Validation . . ." in digital green lettering. It took a moment for Elsa to understand before a slight smile began to form across her lips.

A freckled shoulder appeared as she scrolled further still, blown out of proportion, tiny blond hairs visible in the sun. Elsa wondered if the arm belonged to Sarah. She tapped on the photo, but there was no tag. Elsa clicked on a picture of a license plate, "GETMONEY," and on an image of the zoomed-in bust of what appeared to be an elderly woman, with plump, leathery arms, on a crowded city street, her head floating just out of frame, wearing a T-shirt which read, *Slippery When Wet.* Elsa scrolled down past a strand of hair blowing in the wind, a photo of a scratched knee, a foot submerged in grass. Elsa stubbed out her second cigarette. Though she tapped the photos, the anonymous bodies were untagged, each image a dead end to her searching.

She had a thought which was supplanted immediately by another, so as to appear both simultaneous with and contradictory to the first: *the absence of the girlfriend Sarah Lloyd on Sam's profile was significant. A red flag, the sign of an ending. The notable absence of the girlfriend Sarah Lloyd indicated their love's transcendence, liberating them of the need to (re)assert it through constant projection.* Both and neither seemed true to her, and though Elsa scrolled until there were no more photos, far past what she assumed was the era of the actress girlfriend, she noted a feeling of frustration: the profile elicited her curiosity while rebuffing any closer reading, which only further piqued her interest.

As she put her phone down beside her and closed her eyes, the retinal persistence of the bright light of the screen implanted itself, for a brief moment, on the backs of her eyelids. She inhaled deeply, blowing smoke into the dark, and tried to locate her feeling for the actor-character.

The actor-character returned to the restaurant almost every night. He would sit, sometimes alone at the bar, sometimes with a small group; the faces were familiar, but the configuration was never the same as the time before. Elsa would pretend to be surveying the status of tables in order to see what he ate, to be sure that it was as she expected. His order was the same every time. At the desk in the lobby, she reviewed the menu she herself had typed. *Roast Chicken with Herb Jus and Frites*. She read the description of the dish—*parsley, tarragon, lemon, capers*—and pictured what the actor-character must be tasting, the astringent citrus, the crispy skin, the salinity of fries soaked in chicken jus.

He never called to make a reservation, and so Elsa began to anticipate his arrival without being able to relax into its certainty. The possibility of his dining elsewhere hovered always above her evenings and on the rare night when he failed to show, Elsa felt as if she had been dragged along, counting the dwindling hours as her hope abated. And though she had never been properly stood up, she imagined, as she walked to her mother's car at the end of her shift, that the feelings which coursed through her—disappointment, disbelief, even anger—must have been the same.

Her manager informed her that this happened every summer.

"They quickly find out there's nowhere else to eat in town, and so they're here every night during rehearsals."

"Right," Elsa said, in order to say something.

"Though usually they know to make a reservation."

Whenever the actor-character arrived, Elsa became overwhelmed, though the impending possibility had become the central focus of her evenings. He greeted Elsa with extreme confidence masked by exaggerated deference, as if each time he inquired if there was space for him inside, the fate of his night teetered upon the mercy of her response. She had never once denied him.

There remained something of the surreal in their interactions: each time Elsa returned to the lobby after seating him, she would spend the rest of her night reflecting on the few words of their exchange, playing them over and over again until the close of her shift. As the night progressed, she found herself doubting their occurrence.

The more a particular utterance or gesture replayed itself in her mind, the less certain Elsa felt that it had been as she recalled. *Amazing*, he had said, or so she believed, bringing his hands into a prayer of thanks, his long fingers coming to rest just below his jawline. She recalled a slight bend at the waist as he addressed her, a dark curl tucked behind his ear, a sheepish grin, but the more she fixated on such details, the more implausible they seemed.

One evening after work, she stared at herself in the upstairs bathroom mirror, lifting her hands to her face in prayer, and bowing her head. "Amazing. Thank you so much," she whispered into the house's stillness, the question of the person called Sam's whereabouts floating across her mind.

Elsa watched a story on the actor-character's profile. Pictures of the person called Sam emerged before her. When it was over, she replayed it, reaching out a finger to hold the photos in place so that she could take a screenshot. She zoomed in on these saved images, an uneasy feeling accumulating, having breached the contract of their disappearance.

Elsa waited at the host stand, willing the entrance of the person called Sam, or the actor-character, or even, perhaps, the man or the woman, though she knew the latter to be impossible. As each hour passed, the likelihood of some climax felt imminent, the anticipation almost unbearable, and at the end of her shift, Elsa could not bring herself to depart. She sat alone at the bar and drank a glass of wine and then another. As the restaurant was closing, she made her way down to her mother's car, stumbling on uneven ground.

Elsa downloaded an app which promised to match her with available singles in the area. She set her preferences to both men and women, her radius fifty miles.

Elsa reached for her phone, using her thumbprint to unlock it. There were no notifications. An assortment of discarded mugs had collected over the course of the week—on her dresser, her desk, her bedside table. On one of her social media apps, she searched for the person called Sam. They never uploaded stories, hadn't posted to the grid since April. Elsa clicked over to their tagged photos and surveyed the familiar images. Clicking on the profile of one of their friends, Elsa scrolled in search of more photos of the person called Sam, but there remained just the one.

Elsa opened her Explore page. Stylized images of beautiful people appeared in squares before her. A brunette beamed in a tight-fitting dress, bent toward the camera, a thin strap falling off her shoulder. She looked like a model. Following the link to the woman's profile, Elsa scrolled down the page, enlarging one image after another. The woman knelt down in public restrooms, middle finger lifted to the camera. She lay sprawled on beds, stood on rooftops, sat on curbs clutching bright green juices.

The woman kicked a leg up in vintage washed denim, did the splits in a short dress and chunky boots against a cream studio backdrop. She embraced her heavily tattooed boyfriend, walked her tiny dog in small shorts and big sneakers, posed for selfies. She drank cocktails and wore bikinis on beaches and took pictures of herself reflected in bathroom mirrors. The color of her nails and her cell phone case changed frequently and often matched.

The ease with which this woman appeared to move through the world stirred up a familiar, vague longing in Elsa—it was something adolescent, something distinctly American. Below the woman's profile name was a link which took Elsa to a different app on her phone. The woman appeared to have her own channel on the same video sharing platform where Elsa had grown accustomed to watching interviews with the actor-character. The recordings were uploaded every few months and had titles like "Prepping for Coachella" or "Random Vintage Finds" or "Best Day Ever." The first vlog clocked in at sixteen minutes and fifty-four seconds; Elsa clicked play.

The beautiful woman is in a colorful bathrobe, seated in a modern, white bathroom. She stands so that the camera, placed on the vanity facing her, cuts her off at the chest. Her face and neck float outside the frame before she bends down and smiles at the camera, her hair falling into her face. "Hey guys!" she says excitedly, as if greeting a room full of friends. She tells her viewers that she is currently getting ready for the concert of a musician unknown to Elsa.

The vlogger is now sitting on the lid of the toilet, her head in frame, as she holds up what appears to be a clear cylindrical vessel, reminiscent of a deodorant stick, filled with a candy-pink solid. "So I've already put on this and my moisturizer. This is Milk's—what is it?" She turns the sleek packaging in her hand. "Watermelon Brightening Serum. Love her," she says, placing the object on the counter, out of sight.

Another woman enters the bathroom, her body out of frame. We hear her say to the beautiful vlogger, "I think I'll go get ready and then come back and maybe we can decide what accessories—"

"And glitter!" the vlogger says, interrupting.

"And glitter," the floating voice confirms.

"Love it," she responds, still seated.

The beautiful vlogger stands so that she's once more cut off at the chest and extends her arms out to a body which now steps into frame. Hands are placed on opposite shoulders; the two jump up and down giddily before entering into a long embrace.

The beautiful vlogger leans over the sink and tells us, as she wets her Beautyblender, that she is now wetting her Beautyblender. She sits down once more and traces a beige stick of concealer under her eyes and over invisible blemishes before patting a pink egg-shaped sponge along her jawline and cheeks.

"Just a little bit," she says, announcing the brand.

She brings the pink sponge to her face once more, blending gently with its tapered end. Next, she twists the top off a small white bottle. "Ilia Skin Tint," she says. "The best foundation ever. Everyone's like, 'Oh my god, your skin looks so good. Are you even wearing makeup?' This is what I'm wearing," she says, holding the bottle up to the camera. "It's a super serum. A little goes a long way." She draws thin beige lines along her brow, her cheeks, her chin.

Elsa felt the urge to reach for her phone until she remembered that it was on that particular device that she was watching the video.

Next, the vlogger tells us, she is going to do her eyebrows. With a double-ended brush, she begins to comb each brow, her mouth pouting in concentration. "I'm just going to fill in the ends." With a pencil, she begins to apply dark strokes to the outer corners of her eyebrows. "We're going to lock her in place with Benefit's Clear Brow Gel." She brushes a mascara-like wand through each brow.

The beautiful vlogger takes out a brown-and-gold metallic palette and opens it before the camera to display two creamy squares, the top an iridescent white and the bottom a dark brown. The woman dips her middle finger into the lower square and traces a thin diagonal line along the left side of her face, just beneath her cheekbones, then the right. Dipping into the brown palette once more, she draws a line on either side of her forehead, just beneath the hairline. She does the same along the edge of both sides of her jaw.

"I'm still figuring this out," she tells us. "I've never been a contour queen."

She lifts a handful of products up to the camera: "This is what's next." In quick succession, she applies mascara, bronzer, lip balm, highlighting face mist, two different kinds of cream blush, two different tones of lip liner, and a lip gloss. Before she demonstrates how to apply each product, she extends the vessel up to the camera, her free hand poised behind like a fleshy backdrop, narrating the brand and precise shade.

Elsa brought a hand up to her face, delicately tracing the lines of her cheekbones, her eyebrows, her lips, her jaw.

The beautiful vlogger is now in her kitchen—all slate-gray countertops and stainless steel appliances. "I'm taking you with me to the show," she tells us. "Here's what I'm wearing." She places the camera on the island and takes a few steps back to reveal a long paisley print skirt, knee-high black leather boots with a square heel, a cropped black halter top, and a black denim jacket. "It's going to be a beautiful night."

We are suddenly at the concert. A series of short clips zoom in on a bright stage, as jumbotrons project the crystallite image, blurry in its strange definition, of a dark-haired female singer dressed like a cowgirl, strumming her guitar. The handheld camera turns from the stage to the vlogger and her boyfriend. Elsa recognizes the man from the woman's social media profile. It is the first time he has appeared;

it is dark, and his face is cast in shadow. The beautiful vlogger leans her head on the shoulder of his white T-shirt, a strand of hair falling into her face, and sings along, beaming.

Elsa felt the bubble of a memory threaten to break through the surface.

It is suddenly sunny inside the vlogger's apartment. The vlog has cut to the next day and the woman appears in pigtail braids, silver hoop earrings, a tight-fitting T-shirt, a miniskirt. She films herself, the camera moving wildly, as she walks about her living room. "We're going to go to Echo Park and then vintage shopping, and then we are going to just live our life."

A phone call from an unknown number appeared on Elsa's screen. Elsa tried to recall the area codes for the man and the woman.

"Hello?" she asked. She was met with silence on the other end before a prerecorded voice began to speak to her about auto insurance, which, being carless, Elsa did not possess. She hung up the phone and lay back on her bed. It was Tuesday, just after noon.

Elsa traced the line of her underwear with little intention of follow-through. Her hand slid to her thigh and rested there. She tapped her fingers on her bare skin as if communicating in Morse code, a tic she had inherited from her mother. The urge to shop arose. She exhaled deeply but the urge persisted. She rose and walked to the window overlooking her front yard. Her hand drifted up to the glass and she tapped her fingers once more. The memory of childhood piano lessons briefly floated across her mind. She walked back over to her bed, unlocked her phone, and started when the voice of the beautiful vlogger rang out in the quiet room.

"So today we're going—"

Elsa paused the video. She thought of the actor-character as a means of diverting her attention, but she could feel the urge take root and calcify in her body. Elsa moved her thumb to the phone's screen and scrolled back through the video until the vlogger appeared once more in the sleek white bathroom. She walked over to her desk and reached for an unopened envelope, addressed to her, along with a pen. She sat down on her bed and pressed play. The woman began her beauty routine once more. Each time the beautiful vlogger applied a new product, Elsa paused the video and carefully wrote down the name of the brand and the particular shade. Elsa's coloring was in no way similar to the vlogger's but she ignored this fact as she continued through. Once she had finished, she used her phone to take a picture of the neat bullet-pointed list on the back of the envelope.

The battery life of her phone was dwindling. Elsa checked her bank account. She examined the numbers before her—less money than she had ever possessed as an adult—and she stood and walked over to the chair in the corner by the window, where her shorts lay, discarded from the day before. She bent to put them on, moved over to the dresser, selected no particular shirt from among all the others, and placed her phone inside her bag, along with her wallet and sunglasses. Before exiting the room, she turned back and walked over to her dresser, pausing momentarily before reaching for the pack of cigarettes and the lighter beside it. She tossed both into the bag and shut the door behind her.

Downstairs, her mother was at the desktop computer in the small room which functioned for both parents as office and library. Hearing her daughter approach from behind, she swiveled around to face her.

"Do you mind if I borrow the car for a few hours?" Elsa asked.

Her mother spun to the computer to check the time and turned slowly back toward Elsa.

"Where are you going?"

"The mall."

Elsa watched her mother study her and resisted the urge to retreat to her room. After a moment her mother said softly, as if she were reminding Elsa of a death which she seemed to have forgotten, "But there's nothing there anymore." She added, "Even Macy's closed last year."

"I'm going to Albany."

Elsa noted a deepening of the crease between her mother's brows.

"That's a long way to drive. What do you need at the mall?"

Elsa reached into the depths of her bag and searched for her phone.

"Mom, can I borrow the car or not? If I can't, that's fine."

"Of course you can, if you can't find what you need somewhere closer. The keys are by the door. I just need it back by four thirty."

"Thanks."

Her mother began to pivot toward her desk. She paused and turned back to face Elsa.

"You're really not going to tell me what you're getting?"

Her mother wore an inscrutable smile, and Elsa felt the memory of a former time flicker between them.

"I'm going to Sephora," she said, lifting her shoulders slightly before letting them drop. "And then I'm just going to live life." Elsa felt the strangeness of the phrase in her mouth, its lack of affect rendering it unclear, even to herself, whether or not it had been intended as a joke.

———

Elsa sat in the driver's seat and connected her phone to the car's audio system. A few lines of a song from the beautiful vlogger's concert came to mind, and she typed the lyrics into the search engine on her phone. From there she retrieved the musician's name, which Elsa had forgotten, along with the name of the particular song whose lyrics were catchy enough for her to remember, and opened the audio streamer on her phone.

She clicked on the most recent album and played the first song as she shifted into drive. A slow number with twangs of country began to play from her speakers. She turned left out of the driveway and reached her hand to the small dial on the dashboard to increase the volume. The sun was bright, and Elsa felt into her bag to retrieve her sunglasses, placing them on her face with one hand, the other guiding the steering wheel, as she allowed the music and sun to wash over her.

The musician sang about love, then loneliness, then love again. The song filled Elsa with the desire for an alternate future she began to believe might someday occur. As pastoral greens streamed by, Elsa considered that her thoughts had been so tightly wound around her past that she had little capacity to consider what lay before her, or that time might bring about change.

She had not been to this mall since she was a teenager, yet at each fork in the road, she found she remembered the way. Unable to plan ahead, she felt herself in a state of intense presence. The music a stimulant, Elsa felt buoyant with thoughts of the things she intended to buy, of potential scenarios in which she might wear them, no longer in a state of presence but of abundant futurity. Her thoughts began to congregate around the actor-character and the person called Sam—she pictured their imminent interactions, of which she now felt certain—and her impending beauty, as the three of them became intertwined. The song that she had recalled began to play over the speakers and Elsa accelerated the car beyond the speed limit, as if riding its rapture.

Trees sped by and the empty road stretched before her. She rolled down the windows and felt the wind whip her hair; she reached up to release her ponytail, shaking her head like she had seen in countless films. Turning up the volume further, she began to sing aloud to the chorus—the lines were now those which she had remembered—and felt the urge to shout *Hey guys!* to all her fans. The fact of their eventual existence dawned on her. She had misspent her life thus far overthinking, it now occurred to her, her foot heavy on the pedal, as she took in the warm air and sunlight and pop. Had she wished to interrogate the state of her current happiness, it is possible that Elsa might have stumbled upon an underlying sense of doom.

The mall was less majestic, less a beacon of promise, than Elsa recalled from adolescent memory. She drove along the small two-lane road that encircled the colossal concrete structure, which, once white, was now a dismal gray. Realizing that she was driving without direction, she took the next left into the near-empty parking lot. She would have to search for the store once inside. Reaching to lower the music, she parked in front of the entrance to a large retail chain which spanned the length of a city block. It specialized in household bargains and Christmas decorations year-round.

Elsa entered the store and was transported back to high school—the scent of linoleum under fluorescent lighting—as she made her way past the wire dump bins which lined the aisle in seemingly random succession: discount paper towels stood next to boogie boards, three-gallon ziplock bags next to lint rollers, kitchen towels stood beside variously patterned throw pillows, which were followed by a bin labeled "4-inch Coastal Glass Orb with Shells" ($4.59).

"Excuse me," she said to a man in his fifties, who wore a black shirt with the store's logo on his breast. "Where's the entrance to the rest of the mall?"

"Where are you headed?" he asked.

Elsa paused for a moment and heard herself say, "Victoria's Secret." The words came out lower than her normal pitch, and she forced herself to maintain eye contact with the man as she watched him redden. She had not thought of the brand in years, had not shopped there since high school, perhaps early college. The man hooked his thumbs to his belt loops and avoided Elsa's gaze, glancing down at his leather loafers which squeaked against the floor as he turned away from her to point in the direction of a group of bookshelves meant to replicate the bows of boats.

"It's just that way," he said, over his shoulder.

"Great," Elsa said, smiling sweetly.

The man nodded in her general direction before turning to tidy a bin of rubber flip flops ($0.99).

Elsa emerged from the store and into the mall's interior. An ornamental fountain loomed in the distance as Muzak drifted through the air-conditioned climate. She walked to the nearest escalator, past a kiosk selling cosmetics made of minerals from the Dead Sea—the memory of another kiosk in a different state, the click of a plastic gun as needle pierced through flesh, cubic zirconia thrust into throbbing earlobes—and reached to check her phone as she descended to the mall's lower level. There were no notifications.

Elsa made her way past the lingerie store which she had no intention of entering. The synthetic mixture of various body mists and perfumes delivered her to a different site of adolescent consumption: sensory overload as music blared in the near-dark, the clinging scent of perfume on carpet, posters of topless teenagers embracing in matching denim, and images of golden retrievers on coastal lawns, her mother standing impatiently outside, refusing to enter the store's migraine-inducing interior. She recognized the universal storefront she had been searching for and crossed the atrium, partially lit from two levels above by skylight.

Upon entering, Elsa was approached by an employee sporting the store's all-black uniform, with bright blue eyeshadow and dramatic brows lined in dark pencil. The salesperson offered her a small basket and asked if she needed help finding anything. Elsa pictured the envelope's list of products, its image saved on her phone. She declined the offer, stating that she was merely browsing.

"Let me know if you change your mind," he replied cheerfully.

Elsa smiled and began to walk through the aisles of makeup displays, each shelf illuminated so that the entire apparatus appeared to glow from within. She tried to remember the last time she had worn makeup. Before the rupture, the most she tended to wear was mascara, believing that visible traces of makeup ultimately defeated the purpose of its application. Retrieving her phone from her bag, she opened her recent photos and began to scan the rows of multi-tiered displays for the first product on her list.

Elsa was surprised to recognize most of the brands as she walked past each display, as if finding herself in a foreign country whose language she had once spoken; she pictured the discarded mascaras and ill-advised concealers and bronzers of her past, the empty tubes and compacts lying in the darkness of forgotten drawers, and recalled how a new purchase had been more than just an item acquired, how each held inside its branded packaging the possibility of experiences to come. Elsa felt the reverberation of this same thrill.

Toward the back corner of the store, she came across the brand for which she had been searching. A sign on the middle shelf of the sleek white display read *High Concept, Low Maintenance Beauty Essentials.* On top of the display, next to the thin letters bearing the company name, a rainbow sign read in black lettering *#LiveYourLook.* Elsa thought of how much life there still was to be lived.

The neatly lined rows of products had a playful appearance—the packaging reminiscent of magic markers and gel pens, all white plastic and colorful lettering—that seemed to depart from the sleek simplicity of more established brands. The mascaras resembled soft tubes of paint rather than the customary cylindrical wands. She ran her hand over the cartridges before reaching for her phone to refer once more to her list.

The beautiful vlogger had applied a thick pink stick across her face, and so Elsa searched for it among the products. On the lowest shelf, she found a row of translucent vessels labeled *Watermelon Brightening Serum.* A short description below recounted the innovative technology used to solidify the serum, as well as the various nutrients and vitamins and their promised effects. Elsa opened the sample and lifted the stick to her nose. There was no scent. She had anticipated something cloyingly artificial and was almost disappointed. She rubbed the stick across the back of her hand and lifted it to her nose. Her opposite fingers tapped the tacky substance. She checked the price ($36).

Elsa wandered the store, Watermelon Brightening Serum in hand, and became more brazen with the samples as she went. She applied a GinZing Ultra-Hydrating Cream, followed by a sunscreen she remembered seeing on a beauty blog she had once read regularly. With a small wand, Elsa applied a clear gel to her eyebrows; she applied mascara to her lashes using a disposable plastic brush.

She sprayed too much dry shampoo on her hair and ran her hands through the roots in order to soak up the excess powder. Pumping a quarter-sized drop of liquid foundation onto her palm, she began to rub it into her forehead, her cheeks, her chin with the gentle strokes of her ring finger. The shade was a touch too dark and created an abrupt tonal shift so that the plane of her face stood out in darkened relief against her pale throat, her features somehow exaggerated. She blinked at herself, the blue of her eyes eerily clear and stark against her new tan. Reaching for a tissue, she blotted her face and tried to blend along her jawline.

She applied a red lip (hue: Ruby Woo); she used a sample brush from a different display to apply powder blush to the apples of her cheeks (hue: Orgasm). After smelling various bottles of shampoo, she then moved on to perfume. She began to feel a gripping in her skull: the early signs of a headache.

At the front of the store, she caught sight of herself in the full-length mirror between tiered shelves of nail polish. Elsa moved in closer and felt some central part of herself recede as she approached. Leaning in close to the glass, she reached up with both hands to stretch the skin taut across her face before letting go. Her skin flushed pink through the foundation near her temples where she had tugged. The image reflected back at her felt like a vision from a parallel universe. Tilting her chin, she gazed at herself through downcast eyes and raised her fingers to form a peace sign. She pouted her lips. Elsa detected a shadow move across the background of her reflection.

"You go, girl."

Elsa turned to find a saleswoman standing beside her.

"I was just—" Elsa trailed off.

"Feeling yourself," the saleswoman offered, laughing.

Their eyes met in the mirror. Elsa detected no unkindness. She looked around to see if anyone else had been watching and then back at the saleswoman.

"I don't really wear makeup," Elsa said.

"I can tell. That foundation is totally wrong for you."

"I know."

The two women stood in silence. Elsa turned toward the colorful bottles stacked on the display beside them.

"Do you want me to take that off?" the saleswoman asked gently.

"Yes, please."

The saleswoman moved toward her, her large breasts grazing Elsa's arm. Elsa noted the urge to sink her head into them, feeling her limbs grow weak as the saleswoman led her over to a chair in front of the vanity at the center of the store. She looked around at the empty space and was grateful that it was the middle of the week and that she suffered no witnesses.

The saleswoman pumped a clear liquid onto a cotton round. Elsa closed her eyes and sensed the saleswoman close to her, felt the damp cotton on her face. The saleswoman's hands moved in circular strokes, removing foundation, blush, lipstick. Elsa heard a soft thud in the trash, listened to the rustle of plastic and the sound of the liquid pump, felt the saleswoman's hands return to her and begin their ritual once more. Elsa breathed in the saleswoman's scent: powder—deodorant, she guessed—underneath indistinguishable floral notes. She was acutely aware of the points of her body with which the saleswoman came into contact: her bent knee; the thin skin near her throat, which the saleswoman held with delicate fingers so as to keep Elsa's face tilted upward. The saleswoman worked on her and Elsa became attuned, as if all her cells were rising.

"That's better," the saleswoman said, stepping back to examine her work.

Elsa felt the distance between their bodies and longed to feel the saleswoman's calming touch.

"Can you do my makeup the right way?" she asked, eyelids heavy. A dampness threatened at the corner of each eye, and Elsa blinked it away.

"Of course, honey."

The saleswoman started over, narrating her steps with solemnity.

"So, this will reduce some of the redness.

"This will bring some brightness to the inner corner of the eye."

After first displaying it to Elsa, she applied each product with delicate precision.

"This will just bring a bit of color to your cheeks."

Elsa noted her body's urge to slip into a deep sleep, soothed by the proximity of the saleswoman and her careful attentiveness. Another strain within her fought the impulse, lest she break the spell that had been cast over them both.

"You don't need much, but a touch will give your brows a lot more definition."

Elsa wished to sit forever in the chair, in the mall, in a town that wasn't her own; to remain perpetually in the process of being made more beautiful by gentle hands. The saleswoman's touch, by now coming and going in predictable rhythms, became slowly that of the beautiful vlogger. She pictured a generous transference of beauty, as if the vlogger had decided to bestow upon her a gift for which she was uniquely worthy. After all her suffering, this would be her reward.

"This will make your lips look fuller," she heard the beautiful vlogger say.

She felt two hands placed gently on her shoulders. "You have great bone structure, especially if you learn how to accentuate your contours." It was no longer the beautiful vlogger speaking, but the person called Sam.

Her eyes shot open.

"What do you think?" the saleswoman asked, stepping aside to allow Elsa an unobstructed view of her reflection.

Elsa felt the tears she had held at bay well up and spill over.

"I'm sorry," she said, reaching out for the tissue box which stood among the smattering of products before her.

"Careful, you'll ruin your makeup!" the saleswoman exclaimed.

She allowed Elsa to dab at her eyes and nose. "Are those tears of pain or pleasure?"

"I'm not sure," Elsa replied. "I don't recognize myself," she said, reaching to touch her face. She remembered to stop just before she made contact, her hand suspended.

"It's you under there, I promise," the saleswoman replied cheerfully. "It will just take some getting used to." After a moment she continued, "Let me know if you want to purchase anything I used on you today. This in particular," she said, holding up a large tan tube, "could be really useful to even out your complexion. And it has SPF, which you should absolutely be wearing every day if you don't already."

"Okay, sure," Elsa said.

"Anything else before I go grab that for you?"

"Oh, um," Elsa said, looking down at the pink stick which rested in her lap. "What about this?" she said, lifting it up toward the saleswoman.

"Don't buy that, honey," she said, her voice low. "That stuff doesn't do anything."

"I heard it was really good," Elsa replied.

"Up to you. Should I go ahead and grab you that moisturizer?"

"I'm actually okay. Maybe next time. Thanks for—well, for this," she said, gesturing to her face and glancing once more at herself.

"You're welcome."

The saleswoman had suddenly grown formal.

"Let me know if you change your mind."

She turned away from Elsa to tidy the mess of products and brushes that lay on the counter. Elsa rose to stand and watched her for a moment before walking down the main aisle and out of sight.

Pink stick in hand, Elsa brought up the list on her phone and moved about the store slowly, adding each item the beautiful vlogger had worn to the growing pile cradled in her arms. Once she had found them all, she made her way over to the line of cash registers toward the back. She looked over her shoulder but could not spot the saleswoman who had attended to her.

"Did you find everything you needed today?" A thin cashier with thick chartreuse eyeliner stared at her behind the register.

"Yeah, thanks."

Elsa deposited an array of small cardboard boxes and plastic tubes onto the counter between them.

"Do you have a beauty rewards account with us?" the cashier asked.

"No, but that's okay."

"All right," the cashier said as she scanned each item. "Your total comes to one-hundred, thirty-eight dollars and twenty-six cents."

Elsa briefly pictured her bank account and pushed the thought aside, reaching into her bag to remove her wallet.

"Do you need a receipt today?"

"Sure."

The cashier tucked the slip into the bag and handed it over to Elsa.

On her way out, Elsa grabbed a handful of tissues off the shelf. Entering the central courtyard of the mall, she flicked her wrist and swung the bag full of makeup over her shoulder. She heard the contents jostle within their packaging and craved a cigarette.

In the driver's seat of the car, Elsa took another look at herself in the rearview mirror before reaching into her tote bag for the tissues, and began to wipe away the mascara, lipstick, blush, foundation. Her face was raw and smudged. She turned the keys in the ignition and pulled out in reverse.

That night Elsa began to touch herself. She thought of the saleswoman who had made her over. *Honey*, she thought into the darkness. *Of course, honey.* She pictured the saleswoman's large breasts, her gentle hands. More than desire, the woman's soft flesh elicited in Elsa an impulse to bury herself in the woman, though the urge quickly struck her as oddly childish, the longing more familial than erotic. She briefly thought of the man and the woman and felt herself tense. Pushing the thought aside, she touched herself once more. Elsa turned her thoughts toward the beautiful vlogger and the actor-character.

She pictures them kissing as she kneels on the bed beside them, sliding her hand up the beautiful vlogger's torso. The actor-character traces the vlogger's stomach, reaches down into her underwear. Elsa basks in their collective beauty. The actor-character takes off his boxers and Elsa pauses to remove the beautiful vlogger's underwear. She imagines her smell to be sweet, slightly synthetic, how she had expected the Watermelon Brightening Serum to smell, like the saleswoman who did her makeup and took such care.

The actor-character moves on top of the beautiful vlogger. Suddenly, there is no distinction between her and Elsa, and Elsa feels the actor-character grow hard inside her. "You're so beautiful," he whispers into her ear. "You're so beautiful, honey." He moves over her, rocking her with his steady motion.

It is suddenly the man inside her, the woman's two fingers pressed against her clit. Their mouths meet above her. She is close, feeling a wholeness for which she had spent her entire life searching.

As Elsa came, she pictured the hard red nails of the saleswoman drawing careful circles across her face.

E lsa stood in the upstairs bathroom, products splayed across the counter. Her phone propped up between the wall and the sink, she replayed the video by the beautiful vlogger, pausing at each step to get the makeup's application right. Once finished, she stared at herself. It wasn't so much that the parts had moved but that they now stood slightly differently, as if cast in an unfamiliar light. Up close, the shades were wrong. But it was still her face; she was unsure what sort of transformation she had expected; she began to remove the makeup.

She descended the steps, keys jangling in her hand. For a moment, she had been engaged in action without thought, like the athlete's flow her father went on about to her mother. Her apprehension of the absence of the ticking of clocks and the tingling of limbs was enough to incite their resurgence. But as she turned out of the driveway, she was comforted by the thought that perhaps a shift was impending.

For the first time since the rupture, Elsa scrolled back through the images in her phone, past the screenshots which dotted her more recent months, to the time of the man and the woman. She did not notice the birds outside, or the warm breeze coming in through the screen of the open window, or the faint pain in her trapezius, likely a result of her stooped shoulders. It was strange to encounter her own image in its various iterations from the time before; she had not taken a single photograph of herself since her return home. As she scrolled through selfies, through photos she had taken of others, and photos others had taken of her, the years began to accumulate and cohere, the photos beginning to appear as a sequence of events—of cause and effect—which was only revealed to her in retrospect.

Zooming in on her expression with her thumb and pointer finger, she studied her former self. There was something sinister, she felt, in this dredging up of her semi-recent past.

She came across a video, taken nearly a year ago, in which the man and the woman were dancing in a large, dimly lit living room. Abandoned glasses scattered the tables and darkened forms reclined on the plush cream sofa and leather armchairs. A mirror on the fireplace's mantel reflected the small light of the phone back into the room, though whoever was behind it remained obscured in the low light of the apartment; Elsa assumed it must have been her. She watched the man and the woman twirl together drunkenly, as if in slow motion, their movements exaggerated for comedic effect.

Jazz played over the speakers and Elsa turned the volume up a notch higher, listening to the ebb and flow of background chatter punctuated by the occasional sound of laughter. She tried to recall the space, the evening, perhaps the day leading up to it, but the memory eluded her. Catching sight of herself, she became disoriented; the perspective of the camera had moved to include her. She was seated on a large upholstered chair, legs curled underneath her, a nearly empty glass of wine held in one hand. So she had not been the videographer after all.

Her head rested against the tall back of the chair, her chin raised. She zoomed in on herself. Her features were soft and radiant in the dim light, more delicate than she normally pictured them, as she watched the slow movements of the man and the woman. Zooming back out, she saw herself smile at whomever it was behind the camera as a shout erupted somewhere off-screen. Her gaze turned back to the man and the woman; they continued to sway. Laughter sounded. She watched her former self watch the man and the woman in rapture. She did not look out of place or left out—she had so often recalled feeling too young, too naïve for this particular crowd—but instead sat with a kind of easeful poise.

She put the phone down. It was late morning, and she rose to brush her teeth. When she returned from the bathroom, she scrolled quickly back through the photos, taking screenshots of those in which she appeared to herself, if not beautiful, at least interesting. Despite liking some of them the best, she passed over any photo which included the man or the woman. When she was finished, she uploaded them to the dating app. She left her bio blank and began to swipe.

Pangs of hunger set in, along with a blunt ache in her skull, both of which she ignored as she swiped without truly looking. The more faces she moved past, the quicker her finger accelerated, and she began to swipe left with vigor, as if eradicating the possibility of romance before the images had been imprinted on her, casting faces aside almost before they appeared.

Elsa swiped, determined to reach an end point, to burn through all her options and find herself surrounded by nothing. There was a dullness in her eyes, in her chest—though she did not note it—as her swiping kept its pace.

The face of the person called Sam sailed across her screen. She tried to stop its trajectory, but it was too late; the face of an unknown stranger stood in its place. Elsa was flooded with panic as her blood began to pump and her hands to tingle, and willed the undoing of an act which could not be undone.

Elsa opened her phone's browser and searched the internet. She discovered a function on the app which allowed her to go back in time, as it were, and undo the otherwise irrevocable, to reverse her action and swipe right on the person called Sam. But she would need to pay an extra fee to unlock the service. Elsa checked her bank account. Her heart beat as she searched the internet some more, though she did not note it. She deleted her account on the dating app and immediately set up a new one. Once she had uploaded the same pictures as before, she began to swipe, her slate clean.

Throughout the day and into the evening, Elsa swiped—as she smoked on the roof, as she sat on the toilet, as her mother called her down for dinner and she replied that she wasn't hungry. She swiped left on every profile which did not belong to the person called Sam, and around midnight, she at last came upon it. She lingered, moving back and forth among the images. Most she recognized from the internet, some she did not. She hesitated over one in particular—Sam was seated in a group on the beach, and though everyone in the photo was looking at the camera, their attention was elsewhere. They smiled into the distance at someone outside the frame. The image produced a flash of painful yearning, like homesickness.

The person called Sam's bio read "daddy spoon." Elsa took a screen shot of each photo and then paused, her heart pounding, and carefully swiped right. There was no match. The profile disappeared, as it had before. Elsa went to the settings folder on her phone, enabled push notifications on the app, and placed the device face down on the bed.

Elsa thought of the man and the woman. The three of them had slept together at night, the man and the woman often embracing, a vestige of their life before Elsa. Whenever the time came for the man to turn his back to Elsa, pressing his body against the woman's, she would experience a glimmer of abandonment. As consolation, she would remind herself that she slept poorly with others—that even though she craved the reassuring touch, it made sleep impossible.

One night, the man had turned to her instead, drawing his knees into the backs of hers, wrapping his free arm around her torso. He found her hand and clasped it. She squeezed to see if he was conscious. He squeezed back. Elsa turned toward him, and he stroked the side of her cheek. They kissed with an urgency she had not felt for him before, and desire burned hot through her, made all the more illicit beside the sleeping woman. She wanted him then, more than she ever had, and she resented the woman's dormant figure, whose presence stopped them from enacting their desire as freely as if they had been alone.

Early on, the woman had asked Elsa to name her favorite director.

She sat stunned, unable to recall a single name, and felt the question had been intended to humiliate her in front of the man. She had recovered by turning the question back on the woman, who had replied simply: *Wim Wenders*. Elsa had never heard the name, though she nodded knowingly. Later, she would look it up, spelling it *Vim Venders* in the search bar of her browser.

Elsa brought the man's hand between her legs, where she was wet, and he slid two fingers inside her. The woman stirred; the two of them froze. Silence.

Will you spoon me? the woman asked, addressing the man in the dark. Her voice was groggy with sleep, though Elsa briefly wondered if it was feigned. Had the roles been reversed, an interruption would have been unimaginable. The man paused.

Of course, he said, slowly removing his fingers from inside Elsa and turning to embrace the woman.

Elsa had shifted away from them then, adrenaline and thwarted desire pulsing through her. Waiting, Elsa finally felt the man's hand reach back for her hip beneath the covers. It was the ultimate act of betrayal; Elsa's heart soared; she had won. The man squeezed her, a gesture of reassurance, or perhaps his way of communicating that his longing matched hers.

None of them had ever discussed the incident. But the relationship ended not so long after that, and it now occurred to Elsa that perhaps this had been her final misstep, a line she could not perceive until it had been crossed. The man had left his hand on her leg throughout the night, as Elsa waited, alert with longing, for morning.

———

Elsa searched the man and the woman and found a picture of them together, tagged from the day before. She felt the room around her dissolve, felt the thump of her blood pumping, heard the ticking of a clock somewhere in the distance. She could not feel through these sensations to make out the tingling in her hands and feet, though had she been able, she would have noted it.

———

Elsa wrote an email to her therapist. When she received a response a few hours later, urging her to reconsider, or at least come in for one last session, Elsa clicked to delete the message and so, too, the possibility of reconsideration.

———

Elsa smoked a cigarette and looked out at the humid, gray day, the green before her almost fluorescent in the dim light before the storm, as her hand made its repeated journey from mouth to knee.

Elsa waited. In defiance, she left her phone in her room as she descended to the kitchen, only to feel overcome by a premonition. She bounded up the stairs and over to her dresser where her phone lay next to the pack of cigarettes. She had not received a match. As the hours passed, she found that the person called Sam became for her more and more abstracted. The particular combination of their features, their movements—which Elsa had studied, and which had imprinted themselves on her, or so she thought—began to elude her. And though she tried, she struggled to picture them.

Instead, there was a movement within her—which was not so much thought but felt—as she began to sense that her phone had in some sense *become* the person called Sam, that the two had transmuted and were now indistinguishable in her mind. And so it was in the device itself that she began to invest her happiness. This development progressed without her truly noting it, her hand reaching through space in search of the person called Sam.

She hid her phone under covers and tried to read—something she had not done since her return home, but which now bore the possibility of distraction. But as soon as the symbols on the page began to cohere, she was reminded of her phone's proximity on the mattress just beside her and her hand grasped for its cool exterior. Illuminating its darkened screen, she found nothing at all—or worse, as her chest fluttered in false hope, a white banner announcing the occasional promotional email or news notification—and each time the loss would feel greater than the time before. The hope of a response slipped away as each hour passed without contact, so that her phone became for her a source of resentment and longing. As if it, and not the person called Sam, were the one who failed to give her what she only now realized she so desperately wanted.

In the late afternoon, Elsa decided to take a walk, though the sun was still high in the sky and the humidity filled her limbs with fatigue. Sasha stood expectantly as Elsa passed her on her way out, but she ignored her, carefully shutting the front door. The dog's gaze followed her as she proceeded down the walkway. Elsa was already down the stone steps by the time she turned around and ran back indoors—pushing Sasha gently to the side—and up the stairs to her room. She grabbed her phone without checking it, as if this refusal forgave her inability to part with it, and slid the device into her back pocket.

Once she was on the road, she reached to turn on her phone's notifications and headed slowly in the direction of the hill, the sun in her eyes.

———

Elsa drafted a text to Caro, which she deleted before sending.

———

Elsa searched for the beautiful vlogger on the global streaming platform and clicked on a video which had been uploaded three days prior. She watched the vlogger and her friends get ready for a concert in Vegas. The mirrors covering the walls of the hotel bathroom created an infinite reflective chamber. Whenever the image of the man and the woman together appeared in her mind, her hand shot out unthinkingly to the touchpad of the laptop before her, displaying the remaining minutes, so that the video was consumed in tiny intervals of forgetting.

———

Elsa drove into town, later than her habitual hour. She sped past the fields, a thick sheet of rain blurring her windshield. When she arrived at the coffee shop, wet and short of breath from the sprint across the parking lot, the person called Sam was nowhere to be seen. Elsa reminded herself that it was for the actor-character that she had been searching.

E lsa watched a video which had been recently uploaded to the channel of the beautiful vlogger. When it was finished, another began to play. It was by a different vlogger, slightly younger, less beautiful and somehow familiar. Elsa watched as the woman documented her days: she made coffee, breakfast, returned to the camera, this time in bed, eyes red and puffy. The young vlogger had been crying. She made light of it, recounting her latest mental breakdown with humor. The young vlogger appeared before the camera dressed for a run, and waved goodbye, promising to return once she had finished. She reappeared, confessing that she had not run, having lost the motivation in the time lapse of her solitude. The young vlogger unwrapped packages which had been sent to her as gifts from various brands. She got dressed, alone in her sleek modern house, across the country from where Elsa lay in bed. The young vlogger made herself up, despite—she confessed—having nowhere to be that evening. The rest of the video she appeared barefaced, in a hoodie and short shorts.

At the end of each video, the young vlogger instructed her viewers to lean in as she brought her lips to the camera, placing a collective kiss on the forehead of each one. The first few times Elsa lay unmoving, but as she felt herself lulled, finishing one vlog and beginning the next, she found herself leaning in toward her computer, head bent as if to receive a benediction. She looked down at her arms as a shiver passed through her, watched the fine hairs rise.

As the platform automatically played one video after another, Elsa began to anticipate the woman's routines as if they were her own. So long as she occupied the time-space of the videos, she found she did not think of Sam or the actor-character, or the man or the woman. She watched as the young vlogger tried her best to carry on, as her days always led back to herself. The young vlogger had nowhere to be, had nothing to do apart from documenting this fact; she lived before the camera and made her money doing so, though it never seemed to lead anywhere new.

Elsa shut the laptop and looked at the clock. It was 7:30 p.m. Most of the day had passed, though it was still light out. She got up from bed and looked out her window into the evening. The road peeked through the trees lining the yard; Elsa pictured the asphalt still warm from the day. Hearing noises from the kitchen downstairs, she put on shorts and made her way to the bathroom. Her parents would soon call her to dinner.

An old makeup bag had sat abandoned on the shelf since Elsa's return home. Opening it for the first time, she swept a shimmery gloss along her eyelids. She rinsed her hand under the cold water and dried it on the towel hanging from the hook on the back of the door before opening a tube of cream blush and dabbing it across her cheekbones. With her ring finger, she rubbed the reddish hue into her complexion and stared back at herself in the mirror, tilting her chin upward and pouting her mouth, only realizing moments later her unconscious mimicry: she recognized the pose from all the beautiful women whose lives she followed on the internet. Her hand shot out for the light switch and she stood in the dark.

At the restaurant, Elsa checked the voicemails and made the assigned changes to the drink list and dinner menu. She printed the updated versions and stuffed them into their stiff navy-blue covers; she stood and waited.

"You look different."

Elsa looked up to find a server standing before her with whom she had only ever exchanged a few words.

"Oh," was all Elsa could think to say.

"Did you get a haircut?" he asked.

Elsa could not tell if the server was flirting. She mostly detected sincere frustration at his inability to locate whatever changes he sensed in her presentation. He seemed genuinely perturbed.

"I don't normally wear makeup, I guess," she offered.

"Must be it."

He stared at Elsa, who stood trapped behind the desk.

"You should. You look cute."

He raised his hand to reveal a lighter and lit the candle in front of her.

"Thanks," Elsa said.

He had already rounded the corner into the kitchen.

For the rest of the evening, as Elsa stood behind the desk in moments of downtime, she did not search the computer for clues surrounding the man or the woman. Instead, as each new party entered, she experienced and pushed aside a feeling of deflation. None of the faces belonged to the actor-character or the person called Sam. When her shift was over, Elsa caught sight of her reflection in the glass door which led outside into the warm night. It took her a moment to recognize the image as her own. Driving home, she would recall the furrow in her brow, the hunched slant of her shoulders, a sadness which she believed to lie hidden, but which her body nevertheless betrayed.

E lsa drifted from room to room in the empty house. Seated in her father's leather armchair in the study, she was flooded with the desire to be elsewhere, and so moved to the living room on the far side of the house—the one which was mostly for show—and sat on the stiff floral couch, mindlessly tracing the carpet's fringed edge with her foot. She made a coffee and then a tea; she smoked a cigarette and then another. With less expectancy as each hour passed, she checked the dating app, until it was no longer compulsion which drove her but merely habit, a muscle memory that prompted her to illuminate its sleeping screen every half hour, feeling the rhythms of her internal clock.

Seated on the roof, Elsa lit her fourth cigarette of the day, exhaling into the heaviness of the gray afternoon. Surveying the yard and surrounding trees against the darkened sky, she thought of Caro and of her no-longer therapist and then of Caro once more. She felt and resisted the desire to call her. It had been weeks since Caro had sent the text to which Elsa had neglected to respond. She struggled and failed to recall what her life had felt like, what time had felt like, before the man and the woman, before she had moved home.

The ping of her phone sounded from inside. Without cause, Elsa knew it was a match. The certainty washed over her so that she grew suddenly calm, slowly inhaling the tobacco from her cigarette. She no longer sensed the phone's pull, and instead felt an expansion inside herself, a relaxation of a tension she hadn't realized she'd been holding, so that even after she had stubbed the cigarette on one of the roof's wooden shingles, she sat erect and took in the landscape around her.

Her mother's car rattled the gravel on the driveway. A few minutes passed and Elsa stood to move through the open window, the butt of the cigarette held between her thumb and pointer finger. She walked past the phone on the bed without glancing at it and into the bathroom, where she flicked the remains of the cigarette into the toilet and flushed, watching the tightly rolled paper soften and grow thick with moisture before disappearing from view.

When she returned to her room and picked up her phone, a banner across the screen displayed a notification from the dating app that she had received a new match. Elsa had swiped right only once after deleting and redownloading; it could only be the person called Sam. And instead of surprise or relief, she experienced a sensation of inevitability; it was this that had lain hidden beneath her anxiety. Rather than the fear of no response, it was the fearful knowledge of its arrival that had compelled her body to seek over and over the device upon which this development was certain to be received—a certainty which she only now recognized.

Elsa opened the app to find a small circle bearing the face of the person called Sam. Scrolling one by one through the photos they had uploaded, she felt a solidity emerge within her, as if touching ground for the first time in many months. She placed the phone down.

Part

TWO

Elsa sat alone under the bright lights of the theater and looked around, feeling exposed. Earlier that evening she had dressed for the occasion, channeling a self who had grown distant, and felt the memory of the man and the woman resurface. Having pushed the thought aside, she made herself up in the manner of the beautiful vlogger, leaving unboxed the foundation which didn't match. As she stroked her clothes, she felt the glimmer of a sensation which was, if not love, then perhaps excitement. With a sense of foreboding, she acknowledged this glimmer and had placed her palm to her chest in an effort to steady this unnamable thing. She pictured the person called Sam coming across her photos and swiping right. She wondered if they had recognized her from the restaurant; she still hadn't received a message.

Elsa had arrived early—too early—and sat herself in the near-empty theater. She looked around the rows of seats which were beginning to fill, expecting to recognize the faces in the audience—from the restaurant, from her youth. None looked familiar, and she was relieved to be anonymous among the bodies which began to crowd the space. Turning to gaze up the aisle, she snapped her head back to the closed program in her lap. The person called Sam had entered with a man Elsa did not recognize.

The two settled a few rows ahead of Elsa, near the right wing, and she allowed herself now to stare, watching as their heads bowed toward one another, speaking softly, or so she imagined.

The person called Sam tilted their head back in laughter and Elsa felt a yearning move through her. She longed to draw closer, to be the source of, or at least nearer to, their joy. What she could see of them, she took in—a nod of the head, a turn of the chin, a pause. The touch of a hand on her shoulder caused Elsa to flinch; she stood to make room for an elderly woman who shuffled by. A tall man sat himself in the row before her, obstructing her view of the person called Sam. Elsa leaned forward as the lights in the theater began to dim.

Elsa realized that she had no idea what the play was about. Lifting the playbill, she was unable to make out anything other than the title in the dark. She bent to place the pamphlet on the floor, her hands settling in her lap, and listened to the shifting of bodies readying themselves for stillness. Despite the air-conditioning, the theater was hot, and she found herself surrounded by strange figures—each one emitting heat and odor and oxygen mixed with carbon dioxide.

Picturing all that was porous in herself, all that she absorbed and secreted, just like the bodies beside her, she began to feel ill. The pathway to the aisle was obstructed by knees and elbows—so many knees extending on either side of her—and she turned her head from side to side. The pumping of her blood and the prickling in her extremities made their return, and she longed to reach out for a familiar hand among the crowd of so many hands, but there was none. She felt the muscles in her legs tighten—an urge to stand—but she resisted.

The curtains of the stage drew back and the actor-character stood before her. She did not think of his breath or of his blood or of his heat, and something in her relaxed as the actor-character began to speak: Elsa forgot the endless rows of knees which sprawled out on either side of her; her body softened against the velvet cushion of her seat as she shifted down slightly, her head resting on the wooden back; she did not think of the person called Sam, or the man and the woman, or of her own body vibrating in the dark. And though the actor-character spoke to the entire audience, his solitary figure moving back and forth across the stage, Elsa felt him speaking not only to her, but through her. His words were her own; so were his movements. She watched them unfold onstage from a vantage point outside herself. The only reminders of her particular body were the occasional fluttering in her chest, a tightening of her fists, which she briefly noted before returning her attention to the actor-character.

A man entered from the left and the two began a dialogue, inching toward one another until they grew close. Elsa returned to herself, the spell broken; it was no longer she who moved across the stage. She was both everywhere and nowhere, captivated by a narrative that was not her own. As new characters entered, she listened as they spoke, ignorant of her separateness. She observed, freed from the awareness of her observing, and became invested in the plot without irony or defense. As she laughed as others in the audience laughed, or grew thoughtful in silence alongside them, it was as if all the disparate bodies had merged to form a single unit. A new self, born out of her forgetting—it expanded and filled the theater.

Sarah Lloyd emerged on the stage before her. Elsa sensed reality pressing in, but she rode past it, back into the darkness. Elsa did not think of her as the girlfriend, nor did she think of the person called Sam. Instead, she watched the love unfold between the actress and the actor-character, and Elsa, too, felt love for this actress, for the actor-character, for all the no-longer-grotesque bodies which filled the room.

Her life, like the lives of the characters who stood onstage before her, would turn out all right; adversity would inevitably lead to redemption, loneliness to love. There appeared suddenly a logic in the arc of her story, which Elsa had previously struggled to find. She would be united with the man and the woman, with the person called Sam, with the actor-character, with perhaps some unforeseen other to whom she would make herself fully known. She would be loved, and she would love; it was through the actor-character that she now felt sure of it, emotion pouring through the space in her chest which had so often felt blocked, and she was reminded of the film that had torn something loose in her.

The actor-character and Sarah Lloyd kissed, and Elsa felt herself expand inside their embrace. She kissed and felt herself kissed in return. The hand that grasped the woman's hair with passion was her own, as was the sighing head which tipped back in response. Absent was the desire to turn toward the person called Sam, or toward her neighbors, and Elsa felt herself engrossed in a present that held promise of the eternal; she did not check her phone or hear clocks ticking or take note of the beat of her pulse.

When the lights in the theater came up and the cast came out to accept the resounding applause, Elsa was thrust back into herself as she stood to join the ovation. She blinked, the space suddenly too bright. The anonymous bodies surrounding her began to display their specificity; a woman to her right struggled to stand, overturning her purse and sending its contents rattling across the floor.

Sharp pains shot through her leg; she had not noticed it had fallen asleep. Shaking her foot, she looked around to see if the others had been moved, if their souls had shifted—as she expected hers had—in the liminal obscurity. Once the applause was over and the stage deserted, pairs turned toward one another and began their slow exit, row by row, until the theater emptied. Elsa wondered if the space would feel the loss of all that heat, of all those bodies. If it would miss them.

Outside, the sky was still light, though the sun had set behind the mountains in the distance. Couples mingled in the grass and groups began to form as families and friends found one another on the manicured lawn, and though Elsa longed to stay, she began to walk in the direction of the parking lot. She thought of the actress Sarah Lloyd and felt envious of all the rehearsals, of the dinners, the kisses—real or not—shared between her and the actor-character. She remembered, too, that the actress Sarah Lloyd possessed the love and affection of the person called Sam, and so her jealousy redoubled as she walked slowly to her car. In the distance she spotted Sam standing in a small circle. She turned away, wishing to return to the sensation of being filled by the actor-character, but found she could only touch the empty space where he had been. She checked her phone. There were no new messages. Stooping, she entered her mother's car.

———

Elsa drove Sasha into town and led the dog up and down the main street. She did not see the actor-character, despite multiple laps, and slowed her pace; she began to sweat in the afternoon heat. It wasn't until the drive home, her disappointment like a ringing in her ears, that she realized to what extent she had put her faith in the encounter.

———

Elsa watched the person called Sam nod goodbye as they exited the restaurant and descended down the slope alongside the actress Sarah Lloyd, the couple's steps in sync, hands held. The light was fading; pink dusk outlined the mountains in the distance. Elsa remained frozen behind the front desk long after they had disappeared from sight, into the parking lot below.

———

Elsa searched her browser for the actor-character. On the website of a major publication, she found a review of the play she had seen. She read it once fast, and then again more slowly. The review was luke-warm. She felt something in her stomach turn, but only by a notch.

———

Elsa finished a pack of cigarettes and bought another. She made a coffee, and then another.

Elsa found her mother in the kitchen just after eleven in the morning.

"Morning," her mother said, turning away from the island toward Elsa. She held a carrot in her hand.

"Hey," Elsa said, pausing a moment before passing her to grab a mug from the glass cabinet above the sink. Her mother returned to her chopping, the two women's backs nearly touching as Elsa waited for the machine to warm.

"Do you work tonight?"

Elsa turned to face her mother.

"Yeah."

"I need the car, so you're going to have to see if you can borrow Dad's. Or maybe you could get a ride home from someone at work."

Elsa turned back to the coffee machine and deposited a pod into the upper chamber. The tight puncture of plastic sounded as she pressed the lever. Different coffee options lit up in blue and she pressed the espresso button. Hot brown liquid trickled into the mug. She did the same with a second pod, and when the dripping ceased, she turned to find her mother facing her.

"What?"

"Did you hear what I said?" her mother asked.

"Yeah, can you ask him?"

"I'm sure you're more than capable of texting your father."

Elsa did not respond. Her mother returned to the cutting board, bringing the knife down on a carrot. On her way to the refrigerator, she thought of the man and the woman, where they were and what they were doing in this exact moment. No longer intimate with their routines, it was hard to say. She noted with some ambivalence that this indicated an increase in distance—temporal, physical, emotional. The photograph of the two of them together appeared in her mind as she poured heavy cream from the small carton.

The mug spun under bright lights; Elsa thought of the person called Sam and what they would think of her if they could see her now, semi-employed and bartering for her parents' cars, still in her pajamas at eleven in the morning. She felt the hairs rise on her arms. The microwave beeped, and the familiar numbness spread through her chest. She sensed it was connected—but not identical—to the clocks ticking and the tingling in her extremities and the blood pumping, and she took note.

Passing her mother on her way out, she felt and resisted the urge to reach out and touch her. Elsa did not have the energy just now to investigate the impulse, and instead felt the fog of her mind roll swiftly in. Her mother chopped in silence and Elsa walked out of the kitchen.

The coffee, rather than blowing the fog clean, would only add an additional layer of static to her ruminations. She welcomed the sensation, taking the stairs to her bedroom two at a time.

Elsa sat on her bed and checked her social media accounts. A model reclined on the hood of a sports car, surrounded by the arid expanse of what Elsa recognized to be a particular western national park named after its population of fuzzy, treelike plants. Each time she stumbled across images of this particular species, she was reminded of the elaborate Soundsuits of a performance artist the man and the woman had introduced her to, first as concept and then—once, at an event—as an actual person. Though she had never seen the desert plants in real life, they seemed to appear on her feed with increasing regularity, so that Elsa had the strange thought that even national parks had their moment.

The model splayed across the car reminded her that she possessed no mode of transportation for later that evening. She texted her father.

Hey can I borrow the car tonight?

Elsa checked her phone thirty minutes later. There was no reply. She typed, redacted, and then retyped, her thumb hovering over the send button.

Dad?

The swoosh of her sent message produced a small shock. She turned her phone on silent. Three dots appeared on her screen: her father's typing.

Need the car tonight, I'm afraid.
Can you borrow mom's?

She said she needs it . . .

Elsa waited but received no reply.

———

When her mother dropped her off at work that afternoon, she asked Elsa if she was sure she would be able to find a ride.

"It will be good, maybe you can make a friend," she added when Elsa didn't respond.

"It's fine," Elsa said, grabbing her bag and shutting the passenger door behind her. She pictured walking home, but the small two-lane highway had few lights and no shoulder. The hilly three miles would take her close to an hour in the dark.

Elsa clocked in and checked the voicemail. She logged each message in the spiral-bound notebook—name, phone number, date of reservation, party size—and removed the few cancellations from the reservation app on the iPad. She then began to return the calls one by one, relieved each time no one picked up, her voice rising as she tried her best to project politeness into the voicemails of disembodied strangers. There was no show at the theater that evening; the book was less hectic than usual.

The servers arrived for their shifts and Elsa pictured asking each of them to drive her home, but she could not envision the interaction. She bent down to retrieve the updated menus from the printer on the low shelf beneath the desk and stood to find a server in front of her.

"Did you cut your hair?" he asked.

It was the same server who had noted her makeup, and Elsa felt something inside her recoil at his keeping tabs.

"You asked me that last week. And no. I just don't usually wear it down."

"It looks nice."

He had already turned and was rounding the corner into the kitchen before Elsa called out, "Can I have a ride home tonight?"

He stopped and took a few steps back in her direction. Elsa watched him scan her face for signs of sincerity, and she resisted the urge to retract the request. She felt her cheeks flush.

"Where do you live?"

She told him she was off the intersection just down the road, near the general store. He told her that it would be fine, but that she would have to wait for his shift to be over.

"I know," she responded.

He stood looking at her with anticipation for a few moments, but she could think of nothing else to say.

"Okay," he said finally.

It wasn't until the kitchen door swung shut that Elsa remembered that she hadn't thanked him.

Elsa had no other tasks until the guests arrived. The pines outside the door cast long shadows across the overgrown grass. She felt an urge to take in the air, though the option had been available to her all day, along with the days before.

With the glass cleaner and a rag in hand, she stepped into the early evening and began to spray the panes of the front door. As she sprayed and wiped, sprayed and wiped, her steady motions lulled her into remembrance of past chores—of dish washings and bathroom cleanings and floor sweepings, performed almost unconsciously throughout her life. Since moving home, she had become exempt. And though she had historically dreaded such tasks, delaying their undertaking until the last possible moment, she found as she drew the rag in small circles that she missed them.

A knock on the glass from inside interrupted Elsa's ruminations and she nearly dropped the spray bottle which she had been holding loosely in her hand. When she stepped back, her manager opened the door just enough to poke her head through.

"You don't have to do that. I just did them!"

"Oh, sorry."

"That's okay."

Her manager extended her arm to swing the door further open and Elsa found herself being ushered into the air-conditioned lobby.

"You didn't notice they were clean?" her manager asked.

"I didn't."

Her manager let out an easy laugh. "Well, I appreciate the impulse."

E lsa waited for the guests to arrive. The pixelated backdrop of bluish mountains and purple sunset glowed at her from the desktop. Launching the browser, she searched for the person called Sam, clicked on their social media profile, and scanned the static grid of photos. Nothing had changed. Elsa hit the browser's back button and began to scroll through the search results. Finding nothing new, she clicked over to the images tab and scrolled slowly, though she had done the same the day before.

Elsa moved through photos of Sam on red carpet events alongside Sarah Lloyd, past candid paparazzi shots of the couple—she preferred these—holding hands as they walked down city streets, in light-washed baggy jeans and sweatshirts, past photos from a magazine shoot the two had been in from the summer before, lying on top of one another against a white backdrop in flowing dresses. Elsa could not picture the person called Sam wearing a dress, despite the photographic evidence before her. The following page of search results contained only two images of the person called Sam; both appeared to predate Sarah Lloyd; they wore their hair long and straight. These images were familiar to Elsa, and each time she came upon them, she found herself imagining a younger version of the person called Sam, full of youthful mischievousness and freedom, which she felt the presence of Sarah Lloyd had come to inhibit. Elsa enlarged one of the images. The person called Sam appeared caught in conversation at a gallery opening, their hand grazing the arm of a woman beside them, whose face was turned out of sight. Elsa leaned in close, her forehead nearly touching the screen. She tried to discern the meaning behind the curvature of Sam's smile.

An elderly couple entered the lobby; Elsa stood straight and closed the browser. The woman asked if there was room for two that evening, and Elsa nodded and led them to an empty table, removed the extra settings, smiled before returning to the desk.

Elsa reopened the browser and signed out of the restaurant's social media account and into her own. She scrolled through her homepage without like or comment. Though she spent countless hours on the platform, across multiple devices, she felt reluctant to leave a mark.

She scrolled through the ads which looked like posts and the posts which looked like ads, and paused on an image of a white living room, sun flooding through the windows. Various succulents and green leafy plants were scattered throughout the otherwise empty space. A thick knit blanket lay strewn across a plush white couch. The text beneath the image read, "Need a hug? Try our Weighted Napper." A band popped up at the bottom of the image which urged Elsa to "Shop Now."

She obeyed and was taken to the company website. As she moved through photos of the weighted blanket on various neutral-toned couches, she felt a beating in her chest somewhere beneath the numbness.

Clicking to enlarge the images, she began to scroll through once more. She browsed the various color options, all stylish mono-chromes. Scrolling further down, she clicked to read the reviews. The site took her to a new page, where she began to skim through five-star testimonials. As she read, she noted a strange repetitiveness, scrolling past one "amazing" after another, past all the various uses of "game-changer," until she had the sensation that she was reading the swarming thoughts of a single, collective mind. Each review read as if it were building upon the last, its components the same, only its syntax slightly altered, until Elsa experienced a fissure in the sequence:

I purchased the Napper for my teenage daughter to give her comfort following a shooting at her high school. She sleeps much better with its weight on her (15lbs). I would recommend this blanket for anyone suffering from anxiety.

Elsa closed the browser and looked out into the candlelit lobby. Her vision was hazy, as if she were looking through water. Her finger tapped the screen of her phone; no notifications. She opened her dating app, her banking app, the computer's browser. Her mouse hovered over the empty search bar. A party of three entered through the front door, and she sat them without remembering to ask whether or not they had a reservation.

When she returned to the desk, the person called Sam stood alone.

"Hey."

"Hi," Elsa replied.

The image of herself searching them moments prior flashed before her. She noted the belief that the person called Sam was somehow capable of reading such thoughts, and so looked instinctually away.

"I'm supposed to meet some people here in a bit," the person called Sam said, "but I thought I'd grab a drink at the bar beforehand. Can you hold a table for six in, say . . ." They paused to look at their watch. "Thirty?"

Elsa reached out of habit for the iPad. She thought she heard laughter erupt from the kitchen, though she could have been imagining it. She pretended to regard the list of reservations.

"That should be fine."

Elsa looked at the person called Sam, who waited a moment longer than necessary. They appeared as if they were about to turn toward the passageway that led to the interior of the restaurant but remained instead.

"That's a good book," they said.

Elsa looked to the neglected paperback that lay face up on the desk beside her. It had been a gift from the man or the woman. Elsa searched her brain for the particular occasion, but there had been so many. Books were recommended, films referenced, clothes and objects and affections traded freely. There had been a time, Elsa reminded herself, the person called Sam standing before her, when she had read.

"It's my prop."

"I see," the person called Sam replied cryptically.

"To flaunt my interiority."

Elsa pictured her mind blown clean. Sam laughed.

"Only to reveal immediately that you haven't read it."

"I would never lie to a guest," Elsa replied.

"Or use props to your advantage."

Elsa felt the aperture of the interaction closing, and she wanted to extend the moment.

"Well, who knows. Maybe this is the gentle nudge I needed," she said.

"Happy to help. I like her other books, but that's my favorite."

"That's what—" Elsa paused, feeling a pain in her chest. "That's what some friends of mine said too."

"But you're not into it?"

"It's not that. It's just my attention these days."

Elsa hoped that the person called Sam would say something reassuring, that they, too, felt the ticking of clocks, or the pulsing of blood, or the weight of messes pressing in, but they stood in silence and Elsa worried she had lost them.

"So what do you do all night if not read?" the person called Sam asked.

Elsa searched for something of note which she could present to them, but all she saw was a steady stream of images from the internet.

"Not much," Elsa said, gesturing to the desk around her. "Unless you count stalking exes online."

The person called Sam began to genuinely laugh, and Elsa felt a sense of relief. She willed herself not to look away.

—

Forty minutes later, the actor-character arrived with two other men Elsa recognized from prior evenings. The question of whether he had seen her in the audience of the theater crossed her mind. He nodded and waved his hand—the gesture more a staving-off than a sign of greeting—and walked past her and into the restaurant, followed by the two men, calling over his shoulder that he had a friend waiting for him inside.

Elsa counted out six menus and trailed behind them at a distance as they weaved through the dining room and over to the person called Sam; they were seated alongside a couple at the far corner of the bar. The group assembled and Elsa stalled, straightening a fork on a nearby table, as they kissed each other's cheeks in the European style; none bore the discernible accents as far as Elsa could tell. She approached them and stood at the edge of their small group, though they appeared not to notice her, as one of the men launched into a story about a mutual acquaintance. Worried that guests would arrive with no one to greet them, Elsa looked over her shoulder toward the entryway. She feigned a cough. One of the men said, "It's fucked. He's had a full-on drug-induced psychotic break. He thinks he's in an abusive relationship with math."

Before she could hear a response, Elsa moved toward the other end of the bar and waited. The person called Sam finally looked over their shoulder and nodded in Elsa's direction as they rose to stand, drink in hand. Elsa took her cue and joined them, as they huddled in deliberation, stepping closer to one another whenever a server attempted to pass by with hot plates or a bottle of wine. They were debating their party size; phones were consulted to check if others were on their way, and eventually Elsa proposed seating them at a table which could accommodate two additional settings should the others choose to join.

Though she had been trained to do so, Elsa could not bring herself to carry Sam's Negroni as she led them from the bar to the table by the windows. The party descended and spread out across the table, and Elsa reached around them and placed a menu on top of each setting.

Back at the desk, Elsa opened the computer's browser. She could think of nothing to type. In search of discarded menus, she returned to the dining room and walked over to the station nearest to the kitchen beneath the red wines stacked high on the shelves. A large pile had accumulated next to the terminal and Elsa reached to collect them.

"How's your night going?"

The server who had agreed to give her a ride stood beside her. He leaned back against the station, his arms hung low and crossed, one hand clasping the opposite wrist. He surveyed his tables as he spoke.

"Oh, fine," Elsa replied.

She turned to face the dining room, and the two stood beside one another in silence. She knew it was her turn to ask the same, but resisted.

"It turns out I don't need a ride home anymore, by the way."

She regretted the words as soon as she spoke them. Elsa believed she could feel him flinch.

"Okay, no problem." He shrugged. "I was just stopping by to say hi."

He stepped away from her and into the dining room. She watched him circle his tables, attentive yet unintrusive. The menus were heavy in her arms. He retrieved a crumpled napkin from an empty seat and folded it neatly before placing it back on the table. He moved to a two-top and refilled a glass of wine. The man and the woman at the table smiled at him in thanks before returning to their conversation. He bent to listen and nodded as an older man spoke into his ear. The man held his sun-speckled hand suspended throughout the interaction, his fingers nearly touching the white straps of the server's apron. Elsa turned and made her way to the front desk.

At the end of her shift, Elsa clocked out at the terminal by the bar and lingered before taking a seat at one of the high stools. The restaurant was mostly empty, and she decided that a drink would buy her time. The person called Sam and the actor-character remained seated in the corner by the windows. A woman Elsa hadn't greeted had joined them. She must have snuck in while Elsa was away from her post at the door. The voices in the group were loud enough to be audible from where she sat, but their words were indecipherable, which granted Elsa the illusion of being perpetually on the brink of comprehension.

She ordered a glass of red wine from the bartender, forgetting that she was allowed—in fact encouraged—to make her way behind the bar and pour it herself. If the bartender was annoyed, she hid it well, placing a glass in front of Elsa and making friendly small talk before turning away to wipe down the bar. Elsa drank her wine as the bartender moved about, bending to organize the glass jars full of cut fruit in the low fridges. Whenever a server passed by, Elsa searched their face for signs of friendly contact, but they were still on the clock and oblivious to her. Elsa checked her phone. There were no new messages. Its screen announced the time: 10:15 p.m.

Are you still out? Elsa pressed send. She took a sip of wine and resisted the urge to look over her shoulder in the direction of the person called Sam. A few minutes passed and she checked her phone. Her mother had not responded. *Maybe you can pick me up on your way home?* she added.

Elsa straightened on her stool. A brief flourish of motion in the corner was followed by a penetrating stillness, as if all the air had been drawn momentarily out of the restaurant. Her back remained turned toward its interior. Though it was inaudible from where she sat, in the emptiness Elsa believed she heard the steady ticking of the wall clock in the kitchen. She pictured its second hand's jerky progression, counting the moments of hushed silence which had overtaken the sparsely populated dining room. Though she did not turn to verify, she felt the actor-character approaching.

Rather than excitement, it was panic which flooded in, as she allowed herself to believe that she was the destination toward which he advanced. Her body sat erect, sensing him pass behind her stool and continuing on toward the bathrooms. Once it was safe, she turned to follow his retreat, his long figure disappearing down the hallway. Had she envisioned the scenario in one of her bedroom fantasies, she might have felt dismay at having been ignored. But her reaction was instead one of relief. She turned back toward her empty glass of wine as her hands stilled—she had not noticed they were shaking—and a scene flashed before her, vivid and complete, as if it had already taken place:

Elsa walks over to the table where the person called Sam sits. She lowers herself into the actor-character's chair and takes a sip of his wine. It is as if she belonged, and she joins the conversation seamlessly, reclining back and lifting her hand to the nape of Sam's neck, laughing along at something someone has said. Her fingers come to rest in the short strands of Sam's hair, just behind the ear. She performs the gesture with ease, and it goes unnoticed by all but the person called Sam, who softens and leans toward her.

The actor-character returned to his seat and Elsa caught sight of her own dark figure reflected back to her from the windows, bifurcated by the shelves of bottles which were mounted in front of the large panes of glass. She tried picturing the last restaurant she had been to with the man and the woman but, like all finalities which only reveal themselves to be such in retrospect, it had not stood out to her at the time, and so she struggled to recall it.

"Are you okay?"

The bartender was looking at her with concern, or perhaps it was bemusement.

"Yeah, just tired."

"You should go home and get some sleep. You're one of the lucky ones. You don't have to stay 'til the bitter end."

Elsa looked at her empty glass.

"Would it be all right if I had one more?" she asked, tipping the glass toward the bartender.

The bartender hesitated for a moment, scanning the room around her before turning to grab the open bottle.

"Who am I to deny you?" she asked, offering Elsa a heavy pour. "Let me know if you want more."

Can I have a ride home? Elsa felt the words rise inside her, but before they reached the surface, she felt the impulse lose steam. She thanked the bartender instead. *Can I have a ride?* She turned the words over in her head; she knew she would never ask. Her phone displayed no new messages. It was 10:34 p.m.

As the wine began to take effect, she found herself turning more frequently to look in the direction of the table in the corner. She studied the profile of the person called Sam, noting the way they slouched in their chair, which had been pushed back at a slight angle from the table, how their lifted ankle came to rest on the opposite knee, their leg bobbing mindlessly as they listened. The shadows of the tablecloth were accentuated in the low light, and Elsa watched it ripple each time Sam's knee moved to meet it. With an ache of envy and longing, she heard their intermittent speech from afar, and noted, too, how they rose slightly each time they spoke, so that their back no longer touched the chair. They lifted their drink to take a sip before placing it back down on the table.

Elsa looked to the actor-character, but her attention returned over and over to the person called Sam. She observed the way their hand came to rest on their thigh, how whenever they leaned in toward the others to speak—some witty remark, Elsa imagined—their hand rose too, so that their palm came down on the tablecloth, a gesture of punctuation, before falling back down to their lap.

The other woman in the group stood. Elsa turned back toward the bar and pictured the way the unknown woman would stoop to kiss each person on the cheek. She heard the rise and fall of voices, unanimous laughter followed by a pause, before the small party reconsolidated its borders and was once again enveloped in conversation. She checked her phone; her mother had still not responded.

As Elsa finished her second glass of wine, she sensed once again a shift in the atmosphere surrounding the table in the corner. She turned to find the person called Sam rise. The others remained seated as Sam reached for their phone and tucked it into the back pocket of their pants, ruffling the hair of the actor-character with their free hand. Without turning, the actor-character raised his long arms behind him and reached to hug Sam's torso. They bent to return the embrace, their hands clasped around his chest. *Daddy spoon*, Elsa thought, and she watched as the actor-character let his arms flop down and grasped Sam's wrists, holding them close to his chest. He held them there, both continuing their conversations at the table, until the person called Sam finally released themself and turned to exit.

Elsa stood. "My ride is here," she said, grabbing her phone along with her empty wine glass.

The bartender murmured a goodbye from the opposite end of the bar. Elsa walked into the empty kitchen, nodding at the lone dishwasher and depositing her glass in the rack. By the time she reached the front door, the person called Sam was already halfway down the paved walkway that descended steeply into the parking lot below.

"Hey," she heard herself say, too quietly to be heard.

"Hey!" she called again.

The person called Sam slowed and turned to face her. Elsa allowed gravity to carry her down the hill in something like a run, feeling her weight in her knees each time a foot fell to meet the pavement. She was winded by the time she reached them at the end of the parking lot.

"Can I have a ride?" she asked.

It occurred to her only as she stood trying not to pant audibly in front of the person called Sam, somewhat wine-drunk, that she might get in trouble for accosting a guest in such a way, and she glanced up the path toward the entrance. There was no one in sight. When she turned back, Sam was smiling.

"Well, first of all, hi."

"Hi," Elsa said. "Sorry, I hope that's not weird," she continued.

She searched the parking lot for their car, though she had no idea what it looked like. The person called Sam shrugged and began to walk, indicating with a tilt of the head that Elsa should follow. The two were silent, Elsa trailing behind. A light-colored truck beeped— was it taupe or silvery gray?—its headlights flashing. Though Elsa tried, she could not discern its precise shade in the dark. The person called Sam opened the door and leaned over the driver's seat to clear a pile of loose pages from the passenger side. Through the window, Elsa traced the veins running along the backs of their hands beneath the car's overhead light. The person called Sam deposited the documents in the back seat and then reached over to open the door from the inside. Only then did Elsa realize it had been unlocked, that she had been standing motionless beside it.

Elsa told Sam where she lived. Once they had turned out of the restaurant's parking lot, the two sat next to one another in silence.

The person called Sam kept their eyes focused on the road ahead as oncoming cars passed on the opposite side, and Elsa regarded them in short glances, headlights illuminating Sam's face before abandoning their angular planes to the darkness. Possible statements, questions, jokes arose and echoed in her head, but Elsa was unable to articulate them; as the silence grew, an interruption felt impossible. She knew the answers to most of the questions one might conceivably ask and so could not ask them. As they descended the hill toward the intersection, Elsa pointed to indicate the way.

"My house is just down this road," she said, her voice too loud in the quiet of the car.

The person called Sam did not respond. They turned on their blinker and made the sharp turn.

"I've never been on this street before," they said, slowing.

Elsa let the statement hang in the air between them.

"Right here."

They had nearly reached her mailbox.

"You can pull up if you want. It's a circle."

The car's headlights shone on her parents' empty house. When the person called Sam parked at the base of the steps, Elsa sat for a moment, staring up at her childhood home. She began to unbuckle her seat belt and the person called Sam reached over, as if to touch her, their hands colliding. Sam withdrew and they both apologized simultaneously. Elsa laughed.

"We matched on Tinder."

Elsa was surprised by her own forwardness, but she had felt a door closing and chose to rush through at the last possible second. The person called Sam hesitated, and though Elsa's heart pounded, she was glad for what she had done.

"Oh, did we?" they replied. "I rarely check that thing."

"Right."

Elsa felt her blood pumping, felt the acuteness of her pulse in her hands, etc.

"You could give me your number," she added.

She stared ahead at the small crab apple tree in the front yard, the green lichen on its trunk almost neon in the spotlight of the car's headlights.

"Sure," Sam said. "But you should know I have a girlfriend."

"I know."

"Okay, then."

"Can I ask why you're on Tinder?"

The force held out, pushing her further still. The person called Sam looked at Elsa and smiled.

"We're open. Plus, I've found myself with a lot of spare time up here."

Once Elsa had entered Sam's number, she placed her phone inside the canvas bag on her lap. Her hand rested on the handle of the door.

"Thanks for the ride."

"My pleasure."

Elsa exited and idled for a moment, standing outside the car's open door.

"Good night," she said.

"You too." They paused. "Read that book. And tell me what you think."

"I will," Elsa said. "Or I'll try to."

On her way up the steps, she looked at her parents' window. No one was home. The sound of Sam's truck made its way down the dirt drive and onto the road.

Inside, Elsa locked the door behind her out of habit and stood in the kitchen amid the gentle stirrings of the empty house—the creak of the floorboards in the cooling temperature of the summer evening, the dim hum of the refrigerator—which, had she not been otherwise preoccupied, she might have noted. When she remembered that her parents were still out, she walked back over to the front door and unlocked it. She flicked the outside light back on and stood beside the kitchen island. Her father had installed a Bluetooth speaker in the corner, and Elsa felt the urge to play music through it, but she was unsure what she would do once it had begun. The fishbowl quality of their family kitchen—surrounded by large windows on all sides—filled her with the eerie sensation of being on display, and she felt herself grow self-conscious at the imagined audience which lurked in the darkness outside.

Elsa was reminded of changing as a teenager in her bedroom, the same room in which she now slept, in front of windows that looked out blindly onto black nights, and the strange sense of uneasy excitement she experienced at the thought that, though her country road likely remained deserted, perhaps one of her school crushes loved her back and so had snuck into her yard in order to peer through the windows of her room. Leaving the blinds open, she would turn her back to the window as she removed her shirt, performing modesty for no one. It was this same shyness she now felt, and perhaps also the secret wish that the person called Sam had returned and was parked outside in their truck, gazing at Elsa through the tall windows, and this image stopped her from dancing to music in her parents' empty kitchen. She checked her phone in anticipation, forgetting that the person called Sam didn't have her number.

Upstairs, Elsa stood to flush and washed her hands over the

shallow porcelain bowl. Leaning in close to the glass, she examined her features under the light to see herself as the person called Sam had earlier that evening, the two seated just beside one another in the driveway, Sam reaching momentarily toward her. Or had she only imagined it?

She was surprised to find herself beautiful in that moment, as in moments past. It was not a beauty she felt attached to, nor was it something which felt immanent, but rather she regarded it as a distant fact, external to herself, which she recognized without sentiment in rare moments such as this.

The person called Sam cut through her present once again. Elsa dried her hands and flicked off the bathroom light before approaching the mirror once more. In the shadows, she hoped to approximate the atmosphere in the darkened car, waiting for her eyes to adjust to the dark as she struggled to make out her reflection.

It was no longer seconds and minutes which passed, but persistent thoughts of Sam. Days ended and Elsa struggled to account for them. She welcomed the feeling of floating, as the person called Sam washed over her.

Elsa wondered how others proceeded in the face of such fixations. Work, hobbies, sleep. Fantasies played out before Elsa, unannounced, leaving her vacant body to perform actions which had long grown rote—the making of her morning coffee, the staring at her ceiling as she lay in bed, the urge to pee and its release. Scenarios played out and she tried to diagram them, as she believed they bore a clue to the source of her desire. But each fantasy was quickly replaced by another, and once one ended, she found she struggled to recall it. She was merely aware of the rush of elation or a sense of foreboding which would suddenly fill her body, sensations she noted without truly feeling and that seemed to disappear as soon as she perceived them. She was trapped on a ride of her own making, one which rendered her powerless and mostly unaware. The days passed and, had she thought of it, she would have found she no longer thought so often of the man and the woman or the beautiful vlogger or the tidying expert or the actor-character.

———

Elsa stood behind the front desk and stared into the empty space of the lobby. She thought of the person called Sam, who was now a backdrop to her consciousness. Whenever her mind returned to emptiness, Sam rushed in to fill it.

———

Elsa unlocked her phone with her thumbprint and opened her contacts, scrolling until she found the person called Sam. She tried out several greetings, weighing their significance and tone, until she landed on *Hey*. She began to draft a message which, once composed, she deleted.

———

Elsa searched her browser for the person called Sam, clicking through the familiar images.

———

Elsa sat a party of four. Upon arrival at the table, she realized she had forgotten to bring menus.

———

Elsa typed in the name of the actor-character and scrolled down to the bottom of the browser. She clicked through the search results until she reached the end. On the last page she came across an article which listed "18 Things to Know" about the actor-character. She read each fact and closed the browser.

———

Elsa texted the person called Sam: *Hey.* After a moment she added, *It's Elsa.* She typed and deleted, *How's it going?* She waited for a reply.

———

Elsa noted and resisted the urge to reach out and illuminate her phone, which lay hidden behind the tall vase of flowers on the host stand. She blew out the candle on the desk and searched the drawer for a match to relight it.

———

Elsa's shift ended and still she had received no reply.

The day lay ahead of her, and the one after that, and Elsa wondered how she might fill the time. She was not due back at the restaurant for another two days. Unplugging her phone from the charger by the wall, she began to check her social media. Though she had not searched for the man or the woman in days, she did so now. But the act, which before had brought the terrifying thrill of anticipated pain, failed to elicit emotion. She wondered if progress or "healing"—she put quotation marks around the word as she thought it—was merely a flattening out, a ridding of affect so that one might remain placid in the face of almost anything, a pebble worn down to its impenetrable core.

Elsa desired to feel, and so began to seek through her phone that which might ignite a response. She searched for images of the actor-character and the beautiful vlogger and the tidying expert, but each face left her cold, and so she quickly moved on to the next. As she did, she noticed an urge at the periphery, aware that this searching was meant to distract from thoughts of the person called Sam. Elsa drove into town in search of them, finding instead the actor-character in line at the coffee shop in front of her. As they waited beside one another for their drinks, he smiled and nodded in her direction. In the soft focus of his eyes, she searched for a sign of recognition.

———

Elsa reached for her phone and found a text from the person called Sam, asking if Elsa was free for a drink. She placed the phone face down on the bed.

———

Elsa wrote, *I miss you.* Before she could change her mind, the message had already been sent. By the time Caro replied, Elsa had forgotten that she had texted.

When Elsa arrived at the bar, the person called Sam was seated alone on a stool by the far wall with a drink in front of them. They stood to hug her, and Elsa returned the gesture, her arms wrapping around their torso.

As they embraced, the person called Sam asked how it was going, speaking into Elsa's ear, and she felt a tingle run down her spine.

"Fine," she replied, pulling back. "How are you?"

The two settled on their stools. They were the only patrons.

"I'm good," Sam answered. "What do you want to drink?"

Elsa looked up to find the bartender standing before her.

"What are you having?" Elsa asked, though she could see that it was a beer.

The person called Sam told her they were drinking an IPA, but that Elsa should have whatever she wanted, that the drinks were on them.

"And if they weren't?" Elsa asked. But the person called Sam and the bartender were both looking at her, and neither laughed, so Elsa told the man that she'd have the same, even though a beer wasn't what she wanted. Though the condensation would feel nice, she thought, her eyes adjusting to the dark room. She made out small rivulets running down the side of the half-empty glass in front of the person called Sam.

"I hope I didn't keep you waiting."

"Eh." Sam shrugged. "I had errands to run and was already in town, so I got here early. Don't worry," they said, looking sideways at Elsa, "you were very punctual."

Elsa wanted to ask what the errands were. It was the sort of thing one rarely glimpsed online, and she thought it might flesh out her view of things, but she thought errands were a bad place to start, and she had to choose her words carefully tonight. The bartender positioned the beer on the cardboard coaster in front of her, its head spilling over the edge of the glass.

Elsa asked instead how the person called Sam had otherwise spent their day. Or how they spent their days in general, as she wasn't sure exactly what the person called Sam was doing in her town. Sam laughed and told her that they were writing some and trying to shepherd other projects through various stages of completion, and though Elsa knew more or less the answer, she asked what the person called Sam did for work, and they replied very simply that they were a filmmaker.

"Do you direct?"

"Sometimes," Sam replied. "Other times I help out on other people's work. I do some editing, some writing, and when I have to, I produce.

"But that's my least favorite," they added, after a brief pause.

"How come?"

"Because it's a lot of bureaucracy."

Elsa pictured herself in the time before the man and the woman, in a pencil skirt and blouse, answering emails from an overly air-conditioned cubicle. She thought of the daily email she received from her boss with the subject line "Food Pls," the body of which spelled out her particular requests. Elsa would reach into the drawer where her boss had left her petty cash and descend the corporate elevator to the fourth-floor cafeteria and fill up a red plastic tray with a plate of scrambled eggs or a bagel with a side of butter, and always a coffee with a little cream and sugar; she would ride the elevator up and leave the tray on the small oval table inside the corner office, where her boss would find it upon arrival. In the quietude of the empty room, Elsa would stare out the large windows as the early morning sun illuminated the surrounding buildings, tall shiny towers nearly identical to the one in which she'd stood, fourteen stories above the street.

"That's why I like the restaurant," Elsa replied. "As opposed to an office," she clarified. "Even though I'm technically bound to the desk in the same way." Elsa wanted to turn toward Sam, but it would mean making direct eye contact, and so she clasped her beer above her lap instead and added, "I think it's all the times I get to get up and walk into the dining room. It's not so stagnant feeling. And no one is looking over my shoulder, so I can do whatever I want when no one is watching."

"Such as?" Sam asked.

Elsa once again felt that they knew far more about her than was possible, that they could read her thoughts, that they knew she had searched their name over and over across the internet, and Elsa took a sip of her beer to reassemble herself and said that the particulars of what she did weren't the point, but rather the feeling of being watched, of having to prove that she was earning her wages.

"As long as the tables get seated, what I do in the moments in between is irrelevant," she concluded.

"So it's the feeling of being watched that you don't like?" Sam asked.

"Or the feeling of being stuck in one place," Elsa replied.

"Right. Because I've worked in my fair share of restaurants,"

Sam said, regarding Elsa with mock-wisdom. "And trust me, you're on display."

Elsa replied that she knew this but tried each night to forget it. She asked the person called Sam if they wanted to tell her what they were working on.

"It's a script," they replied, pausing to consider their wording. "A movie script about two sisters who've had, well—let's say, an incestuous event."

"That's quite the elevator pitch."

The person called Sam laughed and, as they did, Elsa noted a shift, as if experiencing a glimmer of a former self.

"Tell me more?" Elsa asked.

The person called Sam lifted their empty pint and the bartender, who had retreated back to the far corner of the bar, nodded and bent to pull a chilled glass from the lowboy behind him, filling it slowly from the tap before exchanging it for the one Sam had pushed forth.

"Thanks," they said, following the man's retreat back to his corner with their gaze, a wry smile on their face. They turned back to Elsa.

"It's about two sisters who fool around one summer when they're teenagers. But the film takes place when they're adults, over the course of a year. And it's about the aftershocks of this—in some ways minor—incident that neither can seem to escape or forget. And one is gay and the other is straight and they both kind of unravel and are sort of still in love, but also kind of despise one another."

Elsa felt her cells rise. She thought of *Persona* and how she had watched it for the first time projected onto the blank wall of the apartment belonging to the man and the woman. It had been part of her education. For days after, whenever the three of them fucked, she pictured herself the blond nurse, nude on the beach, taking the young boy inside her over and over.

"It sounds hot. In a fucked-up way," Elsa said finally.

"Thank you."

The person called Sam took another sip from their glass and turned to face Elsa. They smiled and Elsa noted the way the thin, soft skin around their eyes crinkled. Sam gestured to Elsa's near-empty glass.

"Do you want another?"

Elsa said she did, but perhaps something else, and Sam gestured, again, over to the man, who put his phone down and approached them.

"Hi," Elsa said when he arrived. "Can I have a martini?"

She thought of the man and the woman and of the city she had left and pushed the requisite images aside.

"Gin or vodka?" the man asked flatly.

Elsa replied that she'd have gin, slightly dirty but with a twist, and the man nodded. She finished the rest of her beer in one attempt and set the empty glass at the furthest point across from her. She could not recall what the two had been saying before the interruption.

"Have you always worked in restaurants?" the person called Sam asked.

"Since I was a child."

The person called Sam laughed but didn't say anything further, and so Elsa found herself filling in the silence, saying that the whole setup, even being home, was quite recent, actually. That she had gotten the job at—she paused, having almost said at her mother's insistence.

"The restaurant thing is new," she continued instead, "something to do while I'm home." The person called Sam inquired what she had done before.

"Just office work mostly," Elsa replied vaguely.

Sam called out this vagueness and Elsa couldn't tell if they were flirting or if she was losing them.

"I worked for a publishing house. For the publisher of a publishing house. And then after that I worked for—well, for some artist friends of mine."

The person called Sam asked for their names, and Elsa wondered aloud why it mattered.

"Because I might know them," Sam stated, as if it were obvious.

It never occurred to Elsa that her circles—or her former ones, the ones on loan to her by the man and the woman—could have overlapped with that of the person called Sam and Sarah Lloyd and maybe even the actor-character. Elsa forgot how small the city could sometimes feel.

"You know, when I was younger, I wanted to be an actress," Elsa said instead of answering the question.

"And now?"

"Not at all," Elsa replied.

"Did you study acting?"

"Never."

"Did you go to school?"

"Yes. Did you?" Elsa asked.

The person called Sam smiled and said that they had.

"What did you study?" the person called Sam asked.

"Something like art history and French."

"Et tu parles français?"

"Oui, mais autrefois, pas maintenant, pas avec toi. Il faut que je bois beaucoup plus."

"Oh, I don't actually speak French," Sam replied, and they both laughed.

"But I still sometimes—" Elsa paused to look at Sam sidelong, with a conspiratorial grin. Sam took a sip of beer and angled themself more directly toward Elsa, their knees touching the side of her stool.

"Go on."

"I sometimes feel"—Elsa laughed—"like I'm still waiting to be discovered."

"For what?" Sam asked.

"I'm hoping when they find me they'll tell me."

The bartender interrupted and asked if Sam would like another beer, and they said that they would, and Elsa noted that there had been no hesitation—Sam had not checked their phone or said something noncommittal. Sam had said it so simply, *yes*, and Elsa felt that possibly they were having a nice time. She took another sip of her martini, wanting to catch up; it was only then that she remembered her mother's car.

"This is nice," Sam said, drawing something abstract on the side of the glass. They asked if Elsa dated much. "I can't imagine the dating pool is very big around here. Especially if you're—well, I suppose I shouldn't make assumptions. But if you're gay."

Elsa felt thrown by the not-quite-question and so forestalled an answer. It had always been men before the man and the woman; she was not sure to which category Sam belonged, if either.

"Any horror stories you're willing to share?" Sam asked. "Dating-wise, I mean."

Elsa laughed. "Not really." She looked around, surprised to find the bar still empty.

"The other week I drove over an hour to Kingston, to go on a

date with someone who brought out their phone and started showing me pictures of their gun collection and all the animals they had
killed—I'm not joking, they showed me a picture of them standing
in the woods next to a crumpled deer carcass, and I told them I had
to go to the bathroom, then walked into the motorcycle shop next
door and just started chatting with the guys to kill time before I had
to go back inside."

"So then now's a bad time to—" Elsa mimed reaching for her
phone.

Sam laughed, and though Elsa knew that Sam was in a relationship, it pained her to think of them on a date, making the effort to
drive all that way for some other stranger.

"Was she—or, were they—hot at least?"

Sam smiled and shook their head wistfully. "So hot."

Elsa felt heat rise from her pelvis through her chest, and hoped
that it stopped there, that it wouldn't bloom and expose itself across
her face.

"And the sex?" she asked, and Sam pushed into Elsa's leg with
their knee, very gently, beneath the bar.

"No sex. Not even a kiss. Just images that I can't get out of my
mind, and the sudden urge to become vegetarian."

"What about you?" Sam asked.

"I eat meat," Elsa said.

Sam told her that they'd been inquiring about Elsa's last relationship, and though Elsa knew this, she replied instead that she hadn't
realized Sam considered their short but sweet-sounding time with the
deer hunter a relationship. Sam didn't laugh as Elsa had anticipated,
but instead looked straight at her.

"I went through a breakup a few months ago," Elsa said. She

tipped the remains of her martini and gulped it down. She had forgotten the appeal of substances, of the simultaneous distance and presence they afforded her, as if the buffer between herself and her actions served to further ground her in the moment. "With—" Elsa paused. "Well, with a man and a woman."

She put the glass down and looked at Sam, who seemed to regard her more acutely.

"Like a throuple?"

Elsa searched Sam's face for traces of derision but found instead what appeared to be a kind of openness. She felt herself grow shy under inspection and turned to look at the rows of bottles which lined the shelves behind the bar.

"That's a horrible word," she said softly.

"Terrible," Sam agreed.

"And anyway, it wasn't really like that."

Elsa wished the bartender would see her empty glass and come refill it, fill her up until she was too drunk to drive, too drunk to dread the evening's end, drunk enough to speak French and have Sam understand her.

"They were a couple before I met them," she continued.

Sam asked how long the three of them had been together; Elsa dared herself not to look away when she replied that it had been over two years.

"We lived together. I worked for them," Elsa said.

"In what capacity?"

"She owned a gallery and repped him as an artist. A sculptor. I suppose that's still the case." Elsa smiled faintly, or tried to. "I was their assistant, essentially. Managing their schedules and travel to fairs, and just helping out with general life maintenance, too . . ."

Elsa trailed off for a moment.

"That's really wild," Sam said.

Elsa looked over to see if she was losing them, but Sam sat inclined toward her, as if Elsa had risen in their esteem.

"It's cool, I mean," they added.

Elsa felt a surge of resentment, as if Sam thought this were the only interesting thing about her, which perhaps it was. But hadn't it also been for this, for future lovers, or for a future self, that she had dived into the man and the woman, headlong and unthinking?

"Yeah, I guess it was," she replied.

"How did you meet?"

"On New Year's Eve, at a party. I didn't really think anything of it, but the next day she DMed me."

"Saying what?" Sam asked.

"Just would I want to go see a movie with her, which we did, and then later that week she invited me to a queer drawing class, and then a week later over to their place for dinner, and . . ." She trailed off, as if the blanks were easy enough to fill.

Elsa looked at Sam and recalled the attention she garnered whenever she explained her situation: a kind of voyeuristic, slightly morbid curiosity. But Sam didn't ask the usual, inane questions such as: Didn't anyone ever get jealous, or didn't the mechanisms of sex become overly complex, or wasn't it uncomfortable to share a bed, an apartment, a life, with two people, or didn't she have a preference between the man and the woman, between men and women more generally?

"That sounds really lovely," they said instead, and Elsa allowed herself to feel just to what extent. She could only nod in response.

"Can I ask how it ended?"

Elsa fingered the empty glass in front of her, pushing it forward then back along the wooden bar, hoping the bartender would notice and come save her.

"They broke up with me," Elsa said.

"I'm sorry," Sam said kindly.

"It's okay. It couldn't have gone on forever."

"Why not?" they asked.

It was such a simple, earnest question that Elsa was flooded by the desire to lean over and kiss them.

"No," Elsa said. "You're right. I only say that now, as compensation."

Sam said nothing and Elsa looked over at the bartender, but he was staring down at the illuminated phone in his lap.

"Are they still together?" Sam asked.

Elsa surprised herself and Sam, who gave a start, by calling out to the bartender, who had not looked up once from his phone in all the time Elsa had attempted to make contact. "Can I please have another martini, whenever you get a chance since you're so busy?"

Sam burst into laughter.

"Sorry," Elsa said sheepishly once the man had ambled over. "And yes, they are," she added, addressing Sam's question. "Or at least last I heard."

"My apologies," Sam said to the man, slipping a hand onto Elsa's thigh under the bar. "My date here was just recounting her first lessons in polyamorous heartbreak."

The man scoffed and began to build the drink in front of them. He lifted the stainless steel canister and shook with a vigor he appeared to reserve only for such moments. The three of them were silent, waiting for the clattering of ice to stop. Elsa knew from her time with the man and the woman that vodka was meant to be shaken, gin stirred. Elsa felt Sam's hand on her thigh, bolstered by its warmth, and hoped they would leave it there.

"We're not looking for a third, you know," Sam said, once the bartender had retreated.

Elsa figured it was meant to inject some levity into the conversation, but perhaps the statement was also a warning. She realized that she had forgotten, over the course of their discussion, about Sarah Lloyd and the actor-character and her mother's borrowed car.

The distance between her face and Sam's was suddenly decreasing. Elsa closed her eyes and felt Sam's lips on her own. She softened and reached toward Sam, holding first the nape of their neck and then drawing her hand up into their hair, interlocking her fingers with the short strands for just a moment before Sam sat back, upright on the stool.

"Anyway," Elsa said, feeling self-conscious, looking down at her abandoned thigh. "Tell me something else."

S eated at the kitchen counter, Elsa thought of Sam: a word they had said, a gesture. She wanted them and reached for her phone. After the two had said goodbye, Elsa sat alone in her mother's car, anxious for reassurance that she would see them again.

Sam was leaving in a few weeks; they had told Elsa the night before that Sarah's play ran through the end of the month. Elsa found herself envisioning an increase of affection, of tension, perhaps even a future which extended beyond the time allotted—thoughts she pushed aside as she clicked on the explore feature of her social media app. Photos of strangers, of accounts she didn't follow but which were by some equation deemed similar to the ones she did, appeared before her and she scrolled without truly looking.

After a few minutes, Elsa searched for Sarah, the familiar images somehow strange now that she had gone on a date with Sam. Sarah was pretty in a way that Elsa did not find particularly interesting, but she wished to decipher the code of Sam's desire. Elsa began to look through the girlfriend's tagged photos, moving through them one by one, clicking to enlarge a scene that intrigued her before continuing on to the next. The woman's style, something she had not noted before, now struck Elsa as effortless, even chic. The more Elsa looked, the more she noted a distinct cohesion, a certain relaxed comfort, even a slight boyishness, which nevertheless maintained always a touch of the feminine: baggy jeans and an old T-shirt with colorful earrings and strappy sandals; a loose button-down shirt, worn open to expose a fitted white tank top beneath, a red lip.

Elsa pictured her own clothes, the faded shorts she had worn every day since she had arrived home and the nearly indistinguishable T-shirts, doled out from various sports leagues, stolen from friends, or bought hurriedly. She recalled a time, both before and during the period with the man and the woman, in which she had reviewed herself most days prior to leaving the house, changing a shoe for a different pair at the last minute, swapping one jacket for another.

Elsa put down her phone, closed her eyes, and envisioned moments that weren't likely to come with Sam, seasons they might spend together, trips to foreign places they might take. For each occasion, she found she lacked the appropriate attire. In her former life, had someone inquired as to whether or not she cared about style, she would have responded in the affirmative. It now occurred to her that she only cared at the precise moment when she felt its lack: that is, when she found she had nothing to wear. And in those moments, she was surprised to learn that she cared very much, but only when it was already too late and she should have been on her way.

Her clothes were folded neatly inside her drawers; Elsa lay on her back and pictured them. With a distinct lack of joy, she imagined stroking them and recalled the impassivity she had felt as she fingered each item, how she had almost been tempted to throw it all away and start anew, how she had been on the verge of something, had felt a quiver of excitement, and how the thought, like most thoughts of hers which presented an alternate path, had curdled as soon as it emerged. Taking in the surrounding mess, she had furrowed her brow instead, sighed almost imperceptibly, and begun folding the clothes for which she held no affection.

Elsa bent and reached for her computer which lay unplugged by the wall, feeling a flutter in her stomach which she had not felt for some time.

The names of the once-familiar sites came flooding back. She opened one tab after another, her browser ripe for consumption. A series of former selves unfurled inside her, and she remembered sitting outside her bedroom, no older than thirteen, as she used her parents' desktop to pour over sites which her older cousin had shown her. More than the goods themselves, she desired occasions to wear such beautiful things. It was always some notional future, and never the present as it was, in which she envisioned herself, newly clad. She felt and resisted the urge to check her bank account.

Elsa recalled the articles of clothing on hangers and bedroom floors, clothes belonging to the man or the woman, clothes she had eventually come to know, borrow, and even begun to think of as her own until she had been forced to part with them without warning. The woman had even insisted on buying her a pair of pleated trousers that cost more than Elsa had ever spent on a single item. That Christmas, the woman had peered over Elsa's shoulder at the laptop screen before them, nodding encouragingly as Elsa asked for her opinion, unsure. And though the act of shopping thus connected her to the woman and the brands she had taught Elsa to covet, Elsa also felt herself looking toward a fate which did not include the man or the woman. The possibility of buying clothes that she would wear with the intent of being seen not by them but by another filled her with a sense of progression.

Moving back and forth between tabs, Elsa contemplated what sort of person she might now become. Lithe women appeared before her, and she found it difficult to envision the clothes on her own figure.

She felt the glimmer of divergent futures pass through her, woven into the fabric of the clothes on the screen.

The faded T-shirts offered the promise of activity, of movement, of ease; she pictured herself in vintage cut jeans, strolling leisurely into a secondhand bookstore in a foreign city; the pleated wool trousers bore the possibility of art openings and of fancy dinners—which Elsa had often imagined and only occasionally attended, always as the guest of either the man or the woman, or both. Unsure of what sort of scenarios, if any, lay before her, Elsa moved through the images with a feeling of amorphous desire. She recognized this feeling from the time before: an indiscriminate longing for all potentialities, all occasions, as if the passing of time bore the possibility of a complete departure from the paltry options her life had offered thus far.

Elsa lifted her gaze from the laptop's screen and looked around her childhood bedroom. She checked her phone; no new messages. She began to scroll through one of her profiles, seeking reassurance that she had once had a definable style of her own. With a sinking feeling, she charted the evolution of her taste to various outside influences: this, the persona she had tried on while dating X; that, when she had wished to convey Y; and then, of course, the man and the woman. She shut the laptop and put her phone down on the bed beside her and sunk her head into the pillows. The image of Sam in profile floated before her, the touch of a hand on a thigh.

She reopened the laptop and began to scroll through various women's clothes, clicking to open ones she particularly liked in new tabs, to be examined later, enlarged. Once she had reached the last item of interest, she moved through her tabs. Elsa weighed potential versions of herself. The boxy, blue-striped button-up: Was it something

Sam would wear? Something they would find attractive? Both? Elsa moved on to the next tab.

A tall redhead appeared in a two-toned, long-sleeved yellow shirt, her small pink nipples visible beneath the tight, sheer fabric. Elsa tried and failed to picture Sam in it. The actor-character seemed more likely. And Elsa? She pictured walking by her parents on her way out the door, her hand outstretched for her mother's keys, and exited the tab.

Three or four items remained open in her browser, and she clicked through them, calculating a rough estimate in her head. She nearly closed her browser before choosing her size from the dropdown menu and selecting *add to cart*. She entered her email, quickly enough that she misspelled her name on her first attempt, followed by her parents' address, and leapt up from the bed to locate her wallet before entering the digits on her credit card. She clicked *complete purchase* and her phone lit up on the bed beside her, a brief moment of hope. But it was merely a receipt that had been sent to her inbox.

Her palms grew sweaty in the day's rising heat as she searched the next site in her tabs. She had forgotten the heady, dark tug of a purchase, the brief pause, the possibility of restraint followed by the rush of the fall; the welcome crossing of a threshold and then pleasure. The dread would come later, but never so strongly as to cause her to return an item she loved, never so much so that in future moments she might call on it, choosing instead sober abnegation. And though she rarely drank to get drunk, she understood the opening of floodgates which occurred for others after the first sip.

She shopped and checked her bank account, which had grown in modest increments in spite of herself, and felt the recognition of an insatiability within her, a sensation she had nearly forgotten, and which pushed her, always, further. She knew she would not be sated until she was filled with true remorse, entering the digits on her card until her browser learned to recognize its sequence, had saved its information—until all that was required of her was to enter the security code on the back, the empty fields auto-filling with her data. She pressed *complete purchase* and watched the receipts roll in, only distantly aware of the awaited text from Sam.

When she arrived at the restaurant later that evening, she had still received no word since their date. Standing under the dim lights of the entryway, she felt as if she had arisen from a deep slumber. Dazed and shaky, it only then dawned on her that she had not eaten anything that day. As she stood alone in the quiet calm before opening, she tried to picture the clothes which were perhaps just now being processed, scanned, even shipped, but she found she could no longer recall the items which had been purchased with Sam in mind, projected into an unlikely future.

E lsa stood on the landing outside her parents' bedroom. She had ascended the stairs in darkness, surprised to find them still awake. Muffled voices sounded as she drew closer; a strip of light lay visible beneath the door. She paused for a moment. Just as she was about to turn down the hallway to her bedroom, she took a delicate step, careful of the creaky floorboard at the top of the stairs, and leaned to press her ear against the wooden door.

Her mother was speaking in a quiet voice. She took the hushed tones to indicate distress, or perhaps the constraint of anger, imagining secrets exchanged, worries articulated in private, evidence of her parents' silent suspicion, which she held always at a distance, aware that, if not love, it was at least a form of attention.

She pressed her body in closer, careful to control her breathing. Laughter broke out from behind the door, a sound which she had not heard from either since she had returned home. Elsa walked slowly down the hall, hoping their voices would cover her tread as she made her retreat.

The phone's handset was pinned between Elsa's cheek and shoulder as she checked the restaurant's voicemail. When she was finished, she tucked the notebook away and glanced out into the summer afternoon. She could clean the door, she thought, surveying the smudges where guests had pressed their fingers to the glass next to the metal handle. Or she could bring last night's menu into the kitchen to see if the chef had any edits, but she reached instead for her phone. It took her a moment to absorb Sam's name, which she now read across the small banner on her screen. The specter of its appearance had loomed at the perimeter of her days since their date; she had checked her phone constantly out of some combination of anticipation and habit, and she found herself squinting as she pressed the button on the side of her device, darkening the screen and then tapping to illuminate it once more. The notification remained.

She placed the phone face down on the desk without reading the message and walked through the kitchen and out into the dining room, where servers moved from table to table, placing candles on tablecloths and straightening silverware. They looked up when she entered through the swinging door, some nodding hello, others ignoring her, before returning silently to their tasks or resuming their conversations in scattered pairs.

Behind the bar, Elsa reached for the soda gun and filled her glass with seltzer. She had forgotten to add ice; she dumped the liquid into the sink and used the large metal scoop to reach into the basin of ice beneath the bar before refilling her glass. As she walked past the windows, a tiny spray from the bubbles caught in the light, cubes clinking.

She opened the message from Sam.

How's it going?

Elsa put the phone down and looked at the time on the desktop. She had made approximately twelve dollars so far that evening, before tax. A marked-up menu lay on her keyboard, left by the chef in the time since she had stepped away. She searched the labeled folders stored on the computer for the menu dated from the night before and began to make that evening's changes. When she finished, she would double-check her work before printing out a single copy to be reviewed, saving the document under today's date. She checked her phone again; she could think of no response. Three gray dots blinked below Sam's message and then disappeared. Elsa waited. The ellipsis appeared once again, and her phone buzzed with a new message.

I'm coming in tonight with some "friends." Are you working? Maybe we can grab a drink when you get off.

Elsa put her phone down and printed the menu. The whirring of the machine sounded at her feet and when it fell silent, she bent to collect the warm sheet.

Okay. That sounds nice.

And yes, I'm working, she added.

After reading the words she had sent, she typed and then deleted a smiley face. She typed and then deleted, *What time are you coming in?* She put the phone down and made her way into the kitchen, menu in hand, and stood in silence, her thoughts elsewhere as the chef dragged a finger along each item and its description.

"Looks good," he said, when he was finished.

"Cool."

Elsa walked out into the lobby. There was no reply.

The hours passed and Elsa ushered guests in and answered the phone and recited apologies for the limited parking. In moments of downtime, she scanned the list of upcoming reservations, but she did not see Sam's name, nor Sarah's, nor that of the actor-character. Elsa checked the time on the computer and then, moments later, on her phone. She went into the kitchen to fill her glass from the faucet and returned to find a group of six having filled the lobby. They had arrived thirty minutes early and had to wait, all six of them crowded on the bench across from her desk.

The youngest boy stared at her, his mouth slightly ajar, unblinking. She opened and closed a tab to the site of a global fast-fashion company, followed by that of a major news outlet, without engaging in either. She seated new guests and, finally, the party of six. She checked the time and signed into her personal email. She tracked the packages of clothes she had ordered days prior, mapping their trajectories as they moved toward her, exchanged by unknown hands. There were no new updates; she had checked their progress only hours before. She signed out of her email and back into the account belonging to the restaurant. The inbox displayed a new message, an inquiry about pricing for private dining, which she ignored, closing the browser.

Just after 8:30 p.m., Sam arrived with two women Elsa did not recognize. One appeared quite a bit older than the others, and they were all three dressed in black, though the older woman more elegantly so, her muted ensemble offset with chunky neon jewelry. Elsa wondered if she was an artist. The other woman appeared to be younger than Sam, perhaps around Elsa's age, and was pretty with short, dark hair. She stared at Elsa with a silent air of intelligence. There was something self-possessed and defiant in her which caused Elsa to falter.

"Hello."

Elsa was unsure in which register—the professional or the personal—she was expected to engage.

"How's it going?" Sam asked, taking a step forward.

Before Elsa could reply, they continued, "Nancy, what name did you put us under?," turning to the older woman.

"It's under Steiner."

Elsa scrolled through the list without really looking and bent to retrieve three menus as a means of buying time before deciding she would seat them wherever; she could sort out the reservation later, unobserved. They were silent as she led them to an empty table. Elsa believed she felt Sam's gaze on her back.

"Enjoy your meal," she said, placing each menu down on the folded napkins.

When she arrived back at the desk, she reached for her phone and found a text from Sam.

You're cute.

Elsa smiled, though she did not note it.

The hour passed and Elsa browsed the internet. A few latecomers trickled in, and she found herself walking more erect as she sat them, sensing herself watched by Sam, though she did not look over to the table by the windows to verify. She enjoyed the sensation—even if imagined—of being perceived. From the entrance to the kitchen, as if from the wings of a stage, she had watched the servers bow and speak in hushed tones before making her entrance across the dining room, the dizzying dread subsiding only once she had returned to the safety of the desk in the lobby. But Sam's presence had altered the atmosphere. Elsa began to slow her motions so as to extend her presence on the floor.

Menus had been messily stacked by servers at the station near the kitchen and she stopped to collect them, her back turned to the dining room. Feeling Sam's watch as she paused, she noted the weight of her body, the menus tucked into the crook of her arm. With her free hand, she traced their fraying corners and pictured herself, standing in the darkened alcove, from Sam's vantage point across the room. In the din of the restaurant, she was able to glimpse herself. Or was it a former self, or a future self? An imagined self on display.

She recalled an evening early on, the darkness of the bedroom punctured only by the streetlights outside the curtains. The clothes of the man and the woman, along with her own, were piled haphazardly wherever they had disrobed, like small, stooped figures. The woman had gotten up from the bed while the three of them were intertwined, and the man rose, worriedly propping himself on an elbow and placing his free hand on the woman's naked back, which she gently pushed aside. *I want to watch*, the woman said, walking over to the chair on the far side of the room, set at an angle in the corner.

The man had scooted Elsa silently toward the foot of the bed, lying her on her side to face the woman and entering her from behind. Elsa looked out toward the bureau on the far wall, following the silhouette of a thin vase with a single dried flower in it before her attention moved to the bookshelves.

Look at me, the woman had said to Elsa, who felt suddenly electric.

"Bathrooms?" Elsa turned to find an elderly man beside her.

"Just around the corner," she said, indicating the way with an open palm.

The man shuffled past. The thought of future witnesses, of others whom she might one day encounter and thus emerge, filled her with a sense of hope.

The text had called her cute; Sam was watching her, she was sure of it, and these two truths excited Elsa. She turned toward the room and looked over to the table in the corner where Sam sat, absorbed in conversation.

Elsa moved across the floor toward the lobby. In the hallway, she stopped to regard herself in the mirror, menus cradled high in her arms. The baby strands along her hairline had risen from the humidity of the day and created a halo around her head; the sharp line of her jaw, almost masculine at a certain angle, which used to torment her. But now she was able to envision its appeal under Sam's particular gaze. The relative symmetry of her features, the curving arcs of her brows; she pictured Sam composing the text. Perhaps they had done it as she led them to the table, or as they sat down, typing the message beneath the white tablecloth before turning their attention to their companions.

Elsa's shift began to approach its close and she checked her phone. She sat behind the desk and looked up and remembered to smile as guests departed. A group of four exited the dining room and made their way through the lobby.

"Have a good evening," Elsa said, looking up from the desk.

One of the women broke from the group and advanced toward her.

"That was the best meal we've had all summer."

"Oh," Elsa said. "I'm glad."

"What a lovely restaurant. A friend of mine came here a few years ago and said it was so-so. But we just adored it. I'm sending my son and his wife here when they come up for a show next weekend."

Elsa held her smile, though she could feel its corners flagging.

"Will you tell the chef we said so?"

The rest of the party hovered by the door. Elsa glanced at them.

"Of course."

Elsa checked the restaurant's email, leaving unread a request to book a reservation for graduation that coming May. She would deal with it tomorrow. She counted the months until then—ten—and tried to envision what her life might look like in such a span of time.

When her manager came to release her, Elsa was unsure what to do. There were no new messages from Sam. She realized she had not replied to their text, and so sent a smiley face. In the kitchen, she found the servers gathered around a rack of glassware, polishing as they spoke loudly to one another. Elsa watched their movements—rack, glass, rag, tray.

"Hey," she said to no one in particular, but the servers appeared not to hear her. She moved to the sink to empty and refill her water. She drank it, thinking, and checked her phone. It was 10:04 p.m.

Elsa clocked out at the station in the back and walked over to the bar, finding an empty stool at the end closest to the kitchen. She looked over toward Sam's table. The younger woman looked up, sensing herself watched, and Elsa quickly averted her gaze. The bartender was talking to a middle-aged couple at the opposite end of the bar.

"You done with your shift?"

Elsa glanced over her shoulder. It was the only server who ever spoke to her.

"Yeah."

"How come you're still here?"

Elsa turned again toward the bartender.

"I was thinking of having a glass of wine."

The server walked behind the bar.

"You know you can just pour it yourself, right?"

He lifted a glass.

"Oh," Elsa said, reaching tentatively for her phone which lay face down on the bar. She left it there without turning it over, her hand resting on its cool surface.

"Red or white?" he asked.

"Red."

"Nebbiolo or Chianti? Or wait." He bent down to the cooler to retrieve another bottle, holding it up for her to see. "We also have this chilled Gamay."

Elsa turned her head toward the table where Sam sat, and they raised their eyes to meet her.

"I don't care, you choose," Elsa said, turning back to the man.

He shrugged.

"Chianti, then."

He poured a glass and placed it before her.

"Thanks," Elsa replied.

The server bowed dramatically and walked away. Elsa watched him cross the dining room and wondered if the gesture had been mocking, but she pushed the thought aside and took a sip of wine.

Turning her phone over to unlock it, she opened one of her social media apps, and then another, scrolling without truly looking. A few of the servers were congregated by the station near the kitchen and she attempted to make contact, but none seemed to notice her.

"Hey."

Elsa turned to find Sam behind her.

"Give me twenty or so. I didn't realize this would be such a long thing."

210

Sam spoke quietly, and Elsa felt her body soften and incline toward them.

"No rush," she replied.

"Great," Sam said, touching Elsa's shoulder.

Elsa suddenly felt very tired as she watched Sam walk toward the bathrooms down the hall.

Elsa looked at her phone. She sensed Sam pass silently behind her and return to the table.

Elsa texted Caro, *Hi.*

Elsa texted her mother, *?*, without clicking the link to an article her mother had sent hours prior on the connection between music and mood.

Elsa liked the post of a friend of a friend.

Elsa left a little heart in the comments section.

Elsa deleted the heart but left the like intact.

Elsa looked up from the bar toward Sam, who seemed not to notice.

Elsa scrolled to reread her recent texts to Caro; she had received no reply.

Elsa got up to use the bathroom.

Elsa let down her hair in front of the mirror, turning her head from left to right.

Elsa sat back down at the bar.

Elsa searched her cells to find that they were no longer rising.

Sam's table stood and Elsa turned to watch them exchange hugs, arms reaching for one another, kisses planted on cheeks. She was unsure if she was supposed to meet Sam by the entrance, and so remained seated at the empty bar. Elsa felt her body grow rigid as they approached.

"Feel like swimming?"

Elsa reached for her phone and pushed her stool back to stand.

"Okay."

"You don't sound very excited."

"I just—" Elsa looked around. The restaurant was empty, apart from a couple who sat in the corner. "I don't have a bathing suit with me."

Sam laughed and began to usher Elsa across the room toward the lobby.

"Neither do I."

They unlocked their respective cars. Sam had instructed Elsa to follow, and she backed out of her parking space and waited for them to make the left-hand turn out of the lot. Elsa looked at herself in the rearview mirror and was startled by the vacant stare, her eyes large and dark. She tried to smile, as she envisioned smiling in the near future for Sam, perhaps submerged in a small body of water, but this only made her more foreign to herself. Her mouth was hidden from view; her eyes betrayed no joy. Sam pulled out in front, and Elsa stared into the red-tinged darkness before her.

Elsa turned onto the road, her headlights glinting off the back of Sam's car. As she drove, she forgot her own reflection and instead focused on Sam, accelerating as they did, slowing at the sign of brake lights ahead. The two cars passed the intersection and Elsa's hand drifted toward the stereo, but she held it there without turning it on. Sam put on their blinker, and Elsa responded in turn, as they made their way up the winding country road. She felt Sam's pull and maintained a steady distance, her body intuiting their motions as they drove through the dark. She had run these roads as a teenager, both alone and in groups of loudly chatting girls, and she pictured her younger self and what that girl might think of her now, following a stranger into the night.

Sam slowed to turn onto the small dirt road, and Elsa's foot found the brake, her hands steering always in the direction of Sam. She wondered if they were watching her, if they were as attendant to her presence as she was to theirs. Elsa realized she could not recall the last time she had danced. The thought was interrupted as Sam slowed and pulled over to the side of the road. Elsa parked just behind.

The thud of Sam's door sounded before Elsa could make out their figure drawing nearer in the dark. The two stood in silence, and only then did Elsa notice the crickets.

"Stridulation."

"What?" Sam asked.

"Nothing."

Elsa was grateful for the veil of darkness.

"Feel like swimming?"

"Why not?" Elsa replied.

Sam took a step toward her. Elsa stood motionless, feeling the warmth of the sun still held in the car's metal door against her back.

"Come. It will be fun," they said.

Elsa longed for them to reach out and touch her, but Sam turned instead and crossed the road. Elsa followed; the path to the swimming hole was worn from overuse and rain, causing her loafers to slip on the loose rocks at the steepest point. She crouched down and clung to the shrubbery on either side. Sam was standing by the water's edge, and Elsa skidded down to join them on the flat bed of rocks which stalled the river's course downstream.

"Now what?" Elsa asked.

She took off her shoes. Sam stood beside her, already barefoot, but the two remained otherwise clothed. Elsa longed for a cigarette or her phone, something to do with her hands, and sat down on a large rock.

"Now we swim."

Sam began to undress. Elsa was unsure whether to look or to turn away; unsure, too, of what she desired. She stood to follow suit, hesitating; she had not worn a bra. Sam stood in boxer briefs by the shore, their back pale against the night. The world around Elsa became obscured as she lifted her shirt over her head.

She stood behind Sam, her arms crossed over her chest, though the air was warm. Neither regarded the other.

Sam waded in, the water reaching up to their waist.

"Ready?" they asked, turning back to Elsa with a grin.

"Not really."

Sam did not hear her, disappearing beneath the water in a shallow dive. Alone on the bank, Elsa waited for them to emerge, following the dark shapes of the trees and overgrown grasses that lined the edge of the swimming hole. The faint hum of the occasional passing car in the distance sounded above the chirping of crickets. Sam remained underwater as Elsa willed herself in. She was surprised by its coolness, a sharp contrast to the humid air, and moved in further still, the water now up to her knees. There was no sign of Sam's movements below. Elsa pushed away thoughts of blood pumping and of clocks ticking and instead looked around and up to the road. She both dreaded and wished for the appearance of an interruption, something to disrupt the moment.

Sam rose, sending ripples across the pool, and began to tread at the deepest point near the center. Elsa watched their legs—paler than they had appeared on shore—move in circles beneath the water.

"For a moment I thought you disappeared," Elsa said.

Sam sunk once more beneath the water without responding. Elsa pictured her body in motion, her muscles stiffening in anticipation; she stood frozen.

"Are you coming in?" Sam asked.

Elsa thought of the man and the woman and of messes literal and figurative and of futures which were not likely to occur. Yet she clung to these unlikely futures; her hope that things might change, that things couldn't help but change, propelled her forward. She pictured herself submerged in the cool water, hair slick and damp.

"Are you okay?"

Elsa did not respond. The actor-character rose up inside her as she ran into the water until it was deep enough to dive under. The motion was that of a hand reaching for a forbidden thigh. Submerged, she felt herself grow weightless, unable to make out the boundary between her body and the water surrounding her. She swam in the direction of Sam.

"I'm great," she said, emerging from the cool depths.

Their bodies were close, their legs pumping steadily to keep them afloat. Elsa dipped down again and opened her eyes, but she could not make out the shape of Sam; she rose, seeking air. The two regarded one another for a brief moment before Elsa turned toward the water's edge. She heard a small splash from behind and spun back. Sam had disappeared underwater and began to swim, first toward the shore and then back, without coming up for air. Elsa watched the distorted figure, pale legs and arms foreshortened and strange. She began to grow cold.

Sam reemerged beside her. Elsa thought of Caro and nearly reached out to touch them before tipping her head back to float.

"This is a great spot," Sam said, their voice muffled through the water in Elsa's ears.

"Yeah, I haven't been here in ages," Elsa replied.

"You've been here before?"

"Not since high school."

"I keep forgetting you're from here."

Elsa let her feet sink down until she was upright, the two treading beside one another in silence.

"We used to jump from there." Elsa indicated, with a tilt of her head, the road above.

"I wasn't sure if it was deep enough."

"It used to be."

Elsa found the small, hard rocks with her feet and waded until she reached the shore. Shivering, she sat down next to her clothes. Sam stood by the shore kicking the water with one foot and Elsa studied the sinewy strength of their back. They turned to face her, and Elsa saw their chest for the first time, their breasts fuller than she had anticipated. She feared the evening's end, though its inevitability produced the urge to rush toward it.

Already, she felt within herself an aching for the present moment, anticipating her future longing to relive this evening. The night had already imbued itself with nostalgia; she nearly stood to dive into the water once more.

"Now what?" Sam asked.

"I was thinking the same thing."

Sam began to dress, and Elsa stood to do the same. Ascending the slope, Sam in front, Elsa felt a pressure building inside her to speak, yet no words came.

"We're in a funny predicament," Sam said, when they had reached the crest of the small hill.

"How so?"

"Because I'm staying with my girlfriend, and you live with your parents. And I'd like to go home with you, if that were an option."

Elsa thought of the creaky step at the top of her parents' stairs and of the man and the woman and of the heavy stillness following articulated desire. She took a step toward Sam and kissed them, longer than when they had kissed at the bar.

"You could—" Elsa said, pulling back from their embrace; she let her voice trail off.

"I know. I've been turning it over all night. But I don't think there's a way. I wouldn't feel comfortable knowing your parents could wake up at any moment."

Elsa thought of the first night she had spent alone with the woman. The two had been too timid with one another to do anything but talk. Elsa had stayed up long after the woman slept, feeling the aftershocks of adrenaline and the forestalled urge to make a move. The following morning the two awoke, their shyness somehow gone, their bodies finding each other instinctually, half-asleep. A first.

"I want you," Elsa said, stepping toward Sam. She kissed them gently, parting their lips with her tongue. The crickets sounded and the cars passed in the distance, and Elsa did not note them. She leaned instead into Sam, who reached a hand past the waistband of Elsa's underwear.

"Fuck," Sam said.

"Fuck."

Later, Elsa would drive home alone, the driver's seat damp from her body, and recall the final kiss of the evening, their lips meeting for a brief moment outside her mother's car before parting ways. It was suddenly chaste between the two of them, less heavy and searching than moments prior, and Elsa would reflect on the fact that she had wanted somehow both more and less, on how she had found herself simultaneously despairing and relieved that it had all amounted to only that. How Sam had pulled away and remained at a slight distance, uttering something vague—was it a dismissive "See you around?" or a more promising "See you soon?"—as they made their way to the car.

When she returned home, Elsa climbed onto the roof. She had put on a large T-shirt from her bureau, her underwear still damp from the swim, and lit a cigarette. If she had been spotted from the darkness of the yard beyond, a slight frown would have been detectable as it moved across her brow above the glow of her cigarette. She had left her phone inside, her face absented from the screen's ghostly blue light.

———

Elsa waited for the sound of the delivery truck to disappear down the road before she allowed herself to run downstairs. The clothes arrived in intervals, always in the late afternoon. Some items she remembered purchasing, others she did not. Whether or not they sparked joy, she couldn't say, running her hands up and down their fabric.

———

Elsa vowed not to text Sam and searched her phone instead for the actor-character, lying in her bedroom's warm morning light. She clicked to view an interview she had already watched; when it was finished, she watched another.

——

Elsa considered a return to the swimming hole. Standing at the front door in her bathing suit, Sasha gazing up at her, she found she could move no further.

——

Elsa snuck into her parents' empty room in search of a full-length mirror. She assessed the merits of a particular purchase, not for cut or color, but rather the evocation of a certain mood. When she was satisfied, she moved silently across the room, making sure to ease the door shut, so as not to make a sound.

——

Elsa smoked a cigarette on the roof. *Hey*, she typed, and waited, placing the phone face down beside her. She ground the end of the cigarette into the wooden slats of the roof and reached for her phone once more. *How's it going?* She pressed send and looked out over the trees, her words flung across town.

In the kitchen, Elsa leaned against the island and zoomed in on an image of Sam. It was one of the screenshots she had taken from their dating profile, before their date, before the swim, and she regarded them newly. Rather than her habitual longing, she felt a welling in her chest, a possessive sense of pride and wonder. She recalled having felt the same way as she walked the hour home after her first night with the man and the woman, the streets of the city empty and littered from the night before. In the winter morning fog, Elsa had been struck by the stark change in everyday objects under this new gaze—the soft sheen of the sidewalk, the neon sign of the pharmacy, the golden, half-moon globe outside the subway's entrance—as if the curtain had been pulled back, revealing the world as it had always been, if only she had known how to look. Like the recurring dreams in which she uncovered a hidden room, a secret wing in a once-familiar house, one that had been there the whole time but which she was only now perceiving.

"Who's that?"

Elsa turned to find her mother's face looming over her shoulder, staring down at the image of Sam on her screen. Elsa turned the phone face down on the counter.

"Jesus, Mom."

Her mother walked past her, over to the sink, and washed her hands beneath the faucet.

"Just a question."

Elsa lifted herself to sit on the island, her heels tapping the cabinets that held the pots and pans. She pictured their oil stains, the burnt bits of food baked into their surfaces.

"Dad says there are no innocent questions."

Her mother dried her hands on the rag that hung from the dishwasher.

"That's jokes, darling. No *jokes* are innocent."

Elsa expected her to retreat, but her mother leaned back against the counter to face her and grasped the golden knob of the silverware drawer.

"That woman is handsome."

"Handsome?"

"Are you two dating?"

"Mom—"

Elsa reached to feel for the phone beside her. Pressing the button on the side, she turned the ringer all the way up and then back down to silent.

"What?" her mother asked. "Have I been judgmental in the past?"

Elsa thought of her mother on the other end of the phone when she had called her, sobbing out the whole convoluted saga from Caro's couch, and asked to move home.

The night before the call, the man had texted her, though the two hadn't spoken since the breakup. They had agreed to meet up at a bar tucked beneath the overpass running the length of their borough. The man had been drinking before they met, had possibly drunk more than she had ever seen him drink, and he began to confess. He hadn't been home since the night prior. The word "home" gave Elsa pause. She had not thought to ask where he had moved. They had all broken up, the man and the woman, too; it was her only consolation.

He'd slept with a stranger, he told her, a girl from Tinder, and Elsa recalled precisely how he had said it—*girl*—and pictured some-one very, very young. He had done it, he told her, to get back at the woman. Elsa felt a jolt of jealousy. She looked at him across the table, his face lit from below by a waning candle, his features exaggerated in shadow.

Why was he telling her this? she asked him. Why had he asked her to get a drink? The man wouldn't say. He shook his head and continued to drink, and Elsa had finally looked away, counting the candles, one on each table, inside the bar. When she was finished, she reached out for his hand.

He said that it was nice to see her, to have her hand on his, and that he wanted to kiss her. Elsa said she wanted that too. The night-mare had gone on too long; their life together would be restored, and soon the woman would return. He leaned over to kiss her, his elbows pressed against the table, but before they made contact, he paused and sat back down and said he had to tell her something. *We never stopped seeing each other. We've been living together ever since you left. But it's over. It's for real now, and I'm so happy to see you.*

Elsa recalled looking at her hand still resting on his and feeling that it belonged to someone else. She sat very still. The man told her that he and the woman had intended to stay together; they had continued their relationship in secret; it was the woman who had insisted; she had grown overwhelmed by their life as three, said that it was simpler, cleaner, much better to be two. Elsa had fixed whatever was broken in them, and the woman asked him to think about whether their situation could truly be sustained: Didn't they want children? Didn't they want to buy a house outside the city and grow old together, as a couple? And he had acquiesced.

Elsa looked at the man then, looking pathetic, his head hung drunkenly, asking Elsa to forgive him. Didn't she remember how controlling the woman could be, he asked, how persuasive? Elsa had expected as much or as little from him, as much or as little from all the men before him, who had always struck her as rather disappointing. She had come to expect it of them, and thus to forgive them in advance. But the woman was different. If there had been a choice, Elsa realized, the man's head still draped over his beer, her hand resting lifeless on his, that if it were to be two of them, she would choose the woman, over and over. She withdrew her hand slowly.

With a man or a woman? Elsa had asked. When the man looked confused, she clarified: *Did she cheat on you with a man or a woman?*

A woman, he replied. *Does it matter?* The revelation stripped Elsa of her final shred of dignity. She had taken the man back to Caro's empty apartment that night, a half-hearted attempt at revenge.

"Have I?" her mother asked, crossing her arms.

"Have you what?" Elsa asked.

"Passed judgment?"

"No," Elsa replied. "I guess you haven't."

A line of cars spilled out from the sloped driveway. Elsa found a space behind a white sedan with a Florida license plate on the shoulder—a rental, it occurred to her. When parked, the side of her mother's car tilted down toward the small stream which ran alongside the road. A passenger would have had a difficult time descending from the car into the long, unmown grass, but Elsa had arrived alone. She checked her phone for the time, for a text, for something to do before she made her way up the drive. Though she was familiar with streets parallel to this one, she had never passed this particular house. She looked around, grateful that she was the only one who had arrived just then, and thus spared a walk up the graveled drive alongside strangers, forced to exchange strained niceties. It was 8:30 p.m., still light.

Elsa paused before opening the screen door. She had considered sending Sam a text announcing her arrival, but she had been instructed in their correspondence earlier that day to see herself in. Through the dark living room, she saw a door which opened onto a backyard and heard the faint sound of voices beyond.

"Hey."

Elsa turned toward the kitchen to find the actor-character standing in the narrow hallway, a beer held to his chest. Her eyes had not yet adjusted to the light.

"Hi," she said. "I'm supposed to meet Sam here."

"They're out back."

"Great."

"Feel free to grab a drink before you head out. There's a dwindling selection outside."

The actor-character took a step toward her and turned sideways, his back to the wall, to make room for her to pass through to the empty kitchen. She surveyed the landscape—opened bottles of wine, half-drunk bottles of liquor, a knife and a pile of quartered lemons and limes on top of a cutting board.

"There's beer and other things in the fridge," he said.

They were close enough for Elsa to smell the mixture of sunscreen and sweat on him, close enough that she could have reached out and touched him. She wondered if this was his place for the summer.

"Thanks," she said, moving toward the island.

The actor-character idled at the threshold.

"You're the hostess," he said, lifting a finger to tap his temple, a look of relief moving across his face.

Elsa examined the options, unsure of what she wanted to drink.

"We actually say host nowadays."

"Oh, right. Sorry."

"I'm kidding," she replied.

He laughed, and Elsa pictured the interviews she had watched and wondered if his laugh was genuine. She found she could not look directly at him and was grateful for the distraction of the fridge, which she opened to inspect its contents.

"Funny," he said.

Elsa leaned her head around the door to search him for signs of insincerity but found none and returned her attention to the fridge. Though she performed the motions of contemplation, the objects inside remained unnoticed. She shut the door and looked toward the doorway to find that the actor-character had gone. Alone, she reached for a red plastic cup, filling it with one of the opened whites chosen at random, and made her way out to the back of the house.

Small groups were gathered on the patio and spilled out across the lawn. The actor-character looked up from his seat as she stepped outside. She nodded in his direction and turned to search the bodies for Sam. There were women in floral skirts and others in ripped denim shorts and tank tops; one wore a linen suit. Most of the men wore khaki shorts and soft, well-worn T-shirts or faded polos. Elsa felt reassured by this, the studied unstudiedness of their style, which reminded her of the city and of the man and the woman who had taught her how to circulate in a crowd such as this.

Elsa had contemplated herself in her parents' mirror earlier that evening, the tops and pants which had recently arrived in boxes strewn across their bed. Dust motes had floated above the floor in the evening light as she regarded her silhouette, turning first one way and then the other. She had not wanted to stand out and so had chosen to wear all black, which now struck her as somber, too formal. Clusters of strangers had gathered on the porch and Elsa felt conspicuous as she walked over and placed a hand on the wooden rail, looking out further to where the lawn met the line of trees and formed a small forest. There were no other houses in sight. At the far end of the yard, a few adults and some children were engaged in games of badminton and croquet.

On the sideline of a badminton game, Sam stood in conversation with a person who appeared to be in his late twenties. As she moved tentatively across the grass, Elsa watched them, not wanting to interrupt. She wished she could have approached the pair without being seen, to hear what they discussed without her own compromising presence, but Sam turned as Elsa neared, and smiled.

"Hi," Elsa said when she reached them.

Sam hugged her and introduced the man, gesturing to him with a plastic cup.

"Elsa," Elsa said, as she reached to take his hand.

"What are you drinking?" Sam asked.

Elsa looked down at the plastic cup.

"Something white."

Sam and the man laughed.

"Is it any good?" he asked.

"Not sure. I haven't tried it."

Elsa suddenly pictured a small cap, steel and shaped like a thimble, only larger. It had been part of a cocktail shaker which belonged to the grandmother of the woman, though Elsa would only learn that later. The shaker had two delicate, vegetal-shaped handles and was cloudy with corrosion.

Elsa swirled the plastic cup dramatically and brought it up to her nose. She looked up at the trees. "Limestone." She paused to look at them. They both watched in silence, wearing the same bemused smile. Elsa inhaled through her nose.

The woman had asked her to make martinis early on, setting the necessary items on the kitchen counter before turning back to some cooking-related task. Elsa hadn't seen the jigger next to the liquor, or hadn't known to use it, and so poured what she believed to be the correct ratio of gin-to-vermouth into the shaker's cap. *What are you doing?*

"And something rounder, deeper, like wet earth. Some citrus, too—lime, perhaps, or maybe grapefruit." Elsa took a sip, and swished it around her mouth, slowly. She looked at Sam to gauge the effect and winked. Sam and the young man laughed in unison.

Elsa had turned to find the woman looking at her with a bizarre expression. *Don't use that,* the woman said. *That's what this is for.* She had held up a small object, its bottom the inverse of its top only larger, both sides funneled to meet at the tip. *It's called a jigger. Look inside. You'll see the measurements, in ounces.* Elsa had peered silently inside at the circular etchings.

"Nice acid, good minerals," Elsa continued, after swallowing grandly. "Sauv blanc, if I had to guess. A Sancerre. Could be colder."

"But you poured it, so you knew," the man said.

"I swear to you," Elsa replied, raising her free hand to her heart. "I had no idea."

"I'm not sure if I believe you."

The man appeared to like her. Sam reached for the cup without asking, and Elsa relinquished it gladly—it was an easy gesture, broadcasting a certain intimacy between Elsa and Sam to the man and anyone else who might have looked over. Sam took a sip and shrugged, handing the drink back to Elsa.

"Elsa works at the Black Sheep."

"Oh, I love that place," the man said, pausing to take a sip of beer. "It's the only decent restaurant in town."

"I'm a hostess. Or host, depending on my mood."

The sun had set. Elsa stood in the bathroom and heard the sound of voices, rowdy as the evening progressed. Smiling, she examined herself in the mirror and began to giggle, her hand rising to cover her mouth.

"Stop," she whispered to herself.

She was drunk. Seeing herself as she had on similar nights—solitary moments stolen in other people's bathrooms—she felt the man and the woman waiting for her on the other side of the door. If she were to turn the handle, she would find herself in some unfamiliar living room, at some other party, and they would look up at her and smile. And she would sit near one or the other and sense the heat of their bodies beside her. Or perhaps she would sit at some point across the room and watch them, relaxed and happy, and for that moment feel something akin to belonging. Elsa shut off the faucet.

She looked at herself and imagined it, the sense of belonging. Before them, its absence had gone undetected. If pressed, she could only describe it as a lack—or was it a longing?—which she had gone on enduring.

Words such as *belonging, love, longing* might normally have made Elsa cringe, but her drunkenness flushed out any insincerity. It was that precise state of union between herself, the man, and the woman for which she had been searching, without truly believing in its existence, all her life. She reached to dry her hands on the washcloth which hung beside the sink.

Outside, she returned to the circular table where she had been sitting next to Sam. She picked up what she took to be her drink among the other emptied and half-empty cups. The actor-character sat across from her smoking a cigarette, deep in conversation with an older man beside him. Elsa watched his face move from light to darkness as he leaned in and out of the shadow cast by a large woman on his opposite side. He inhaled and let the hand holding his cigarette fall to rest on the table. Elsa studied his fingers, long and elegant, and imagined a current which flowed through them, producing a jolt on each object, each body they touched.

Sam's arm grazed Elsa's own and she turned toward them, but the motion had been mindless; Sam was engaged in a conversation which Elsa could not quite follow with a woman across the table. It had grown late; the families and children had gone home, and only a small group remained, congregated on the porch. Elsa was still unsure whose house this was. As she reached for a cigarette from her bag, she took another sip of gin, which she had mixed earlier with tonic. Not knowing where to look, she feigned deep contemplation in the direction of the shadows beyond the porch as she drew the lighter up. She listened for the sound of cars in the distance but was unable to hear the road above the chatter and the music. A song issued from the portable speaker on the far side of the porch; she wondered if it had been playing the whole time.

All evening, Elsa had wished to inquire about Sarah's absence, but she hadn't found a moment alone with Sam. She had come to the conclusion after her first sips of wine on the lawn that no answer would satisfy her; now, drunk, the answer no longer mattered.

Another sip of gin and she felt the expansion. Coasting atop it, she decided she would ride the wave wherever it took her and looked around, her vision flickering from one detail to the next—a vape which someone had lodged between two slats of the wooden table, the small china plate which served as a makeshift ashtray, the light fixture just outside the door to the porch and the swarm of moths which flung their small bodies against it, relentless. Focusing first on one face, then another, she grew bolder, lingering longer with each sip she took. She smiled, if not directly at the actor-character, then in his general direction, but he remained attentive to his companion.

"I like your bracelet," she said, leaning over to a woman near her who was, like Elsa, caught between two conversations on either side, a part of neither.

"Thanks," the woman said brightly. For a brief instant, hope vibrated in the air between them. Each regarded the other in anticipation, but neither appeared to think of anything else to say.

Leaning back in her chair, Elsa took the final drag from her cigarette and closed her eyes; it made her dizzy. The steady inflections of Sam's voice continued beside her, their body growing farther and then nearer as they spoke. Each time Sam returned to rest, arm just barely touching hers, Elsa felt herself grow soft. *Sam*, she thought, turning the name over in her head.

"You okay?"

The table had grown quiet. Elsa opened her eyes; shadowed faces stared at her.

"Yes," she replied. In an attempt not to slur, her speech was brisk, almost formal. She turned to find Sam smiling at her.

"Looks like someone's going to need a ride home." Sam laughed.

She had forgotten that she had driven to the party and would presumably have to get herself home.

"Maybe it's time for that swim."

Elsa looked up. It was the actor-character who had spoken.

The group piled into someone's car, Elsa among them. The actor-character sat in the passenger seat beside an older man who drove them along familiar roads which felt strange in this new context. Their discussions turned to the play, and Elsa listened from the back seat. She had been about to ask how they all knew each other but the answer quickly became evident, and there was nothing left for her to contribute. Feeling her presence recede, she was glad for it. Sam leaned into her at each turn, their legs and arms touching. Each time they righted themself in the middle seat, Elsa found that she missed them, anticipating the next turn, an occasion for contact. Placing her forehead against the glass of the back window, she looked out at the passing trees.

Elsa thought of love. First it was just the word. *Love*, she had thought, as she attempted to focus on an individual blade of tall grass beneath a streetlight before it disappeared from sight. As Sam's leg touched hers and moved away, she thought, *merging*. She could not help it. She was ripe and shapeless, in awe of the sharp edges of others who struck her as alien and complete. At the invitation of the man and the woman, she had leapt without hesitation, allowing herself to flow into their lives like raw material into a mold. Sam leaned into her as the car halted at the town's sole streetlight. Even when the objects of her affection moved as close to her as another body could, it had never sufficed. It was this insatiability that unnerved her; she felt unable to combat it. It occurred to her that she had at times been unhappy with the man and the woman.

"I'm not sure I caught your name."

Elsa's forehead was still pressed against the window and it took her a moment to realize she had been addressed by the woman seated on the far side of the back seat.

Elsa leaned back. The car had grown silent.

"Elsa."

"Like the movie," the actor-character said, and the others in the car laughed.

"What movie?" she asked.

"Which way?" the driver asked as they approached the intersection.

The actor-character indicated the turn, and it seemed Elsa's question had been forgotten. It occurred to her that she had not checked her phone since she had arrived at the party. She reached for it, realizing only then that she had left it in her bag back at the house.

From the edge of the shore, Elsa watched the bodies in the river, her feet submerged in the shallow water. Another car full of people had joined their group, some jumping straight in, while others hovered on the bank. It had by now become apparent that those who remained had worked together on the show. They were bonded by this fact, and Elsa stood apart and watched them as they splashed and joked, wondering once more where Sarah was.

"When do you leave?" she heard one person ask another, the two standing waist-deep a few yards in front of her.

"Tomorrow. What about you?"

"Monday."

Elsa remembered that Sam, too, was leaving. Perhaps as soon as that weekend. She felt the urge to search for a phone which was not there, and focused instead on the streetlights glinting off the river as she removed her pants and then her shirt. She was topless, but so were the others. Ignoring the cold, she waded in, arms crossed over her chest. Once it was deep enough, she began to swim. She would have liked to allow her body to grow pliant, to let the gentle current lead her downstream toward some other fate, but she took a deep breath and ducked her head under, her hair floating above her, weightless and soft. Rising for air, she wiped the water from her eyes and looked for Sam. Beyond the semi-familiar bodies, Elsa saw them seated beside the actor-character on a cluster of rocks on the far shore and began to swim in their direction. The cold water had a minor sobering effect, though Elsa was dimly aware as she swam across the river that she would not have been so bold as to approach them had she not been inebriated. She tried to recall, her arms gliding in slow strokes, if she had ever swum drunk before.

The water grew shallow, and she felt the rocks beneath her feet, moving to join the two on their perch. They grew silent as soon as she was in earshot, and though Sam placed a hand on Elsa's back as she lowered herself to sit, Elsa had the sense that she had interrupted something between them. She wondered if Sam had ever been with men, if the palpable connection between them and the actor-character was, if not romantic, then perhaps erotic.

The three sat without speaking and watched the others swim. Across the shore, where clothes were strewn along the trunk of a long-fallen tree, Elsa saw the twin lights of cigarettes ignite in the dark. She could only trace the outlines of the two figures attached. She listened to the river's current, steady against the sound of voices, magnified by alcohol and the reverberative effects of the water.

"When do you leave?" she asked.

"The day after tomorrow," Sam replied.

Elsa felt their hand leave her.

"Is the play over?"

"Last night was our final," the actor-character said. "Thank god," he added.

The two laughed.

"You didn't like it?" Elsa asked, looking first at the actor-character and then back to Sam.

"It was fine," he replied.

Elsa felt that her presence had made him reticent and that there was more to what he said. Bodies began to congregate on the shore across the water. She tried to locate the orange tinge of the cigarettes, but they had disappeared.

"I saw it," Elsa said. "You were good."

"I didn't know that," Sam said.

Elsa felt their gaze on her but kept her own steady on the opposite shore, worried she had spoken out of turn. Was the silence which had befallen the three of them easy or expectant? Elsa began to shiver.

"Cold?"

"A little," she replied.

"Shall we?" Sam asked.

"Race you," the actor-character called out, running into the water. Elsa and Sam watched him swim toward the opposite bank.

On the way back, Elsa swam slowly with her head above water, keeping her eyes on Sam out in front of her. Each time their arms cut through the surface of the water, Elsa felt a strange sadness. When Sam reached the bank and rose to their feet, they did not look back in search of Elsa.

Back at the house, the small group that remained was seated in the living room. Those who had swum dispersed to various bathrooms to change, and Elsa stood in the hall by the kitchen. She felt herself grow heavy with the knowledge that the night would soon end, and she checked the time on her phone. Searching the room for the actor-character, she found him seated on a folding chair in the corner; the predictable sensations failed to materialize. All that persisted was a hollow curiosity, a desire to explore a particular possibility if only to placate a former self. She had lain in her childhood bedroom and conjured evenings such as this, but in her imaginings there had always been a spark between herself and the actor-character. Leaning against the wall, she found that the fantasy no longer held. In person, she found him slippery. Or perhaps it was her. Their interactions had failed to accumulate into anything greater than a cluster of phrases. She looked around the room for Sam.

When the downstairs bathroom was free, Elsa entered and locked the door behind her. She tossed her wet underwear into her bag and pulled her pants over her hips. She dried her hair on the towel which hung on the back of the door. With wet hands, she rubbed the thin skin beneath her eyes, darkened by mascara, and stepped back from her reflection, no longer so drunk. Sam was leaving the day after next. Voices sounded beyond the door. It occurred to her that those, too, would soon be gone.

She knelt down onto the wet bathmat and clutched the side of the small tub. Images of Caro and the woman from the mall pressed in on her, and she longed to return to prior moments of release. She opened her mouth, willing a sob, but nothing came out. She stood and looked at herself once more. Without thinking, she stuck two fingers down her throat and gagged a milky substance into the toilet. It was mostly liquid; she felt purified.

She bent over to drink from the tap, swirling the water around before spitting it out into the basin, and watched it slide slowly down the drain.

When she left the bathroom, Sam was standing outside the door.

"Hey."

"Hi."

"I just have to pee quickly, but then do you want to get out of here?"

"Yes," Elsa replied, stepping aside to let them pass.

On the road, Elsa watched the gentle curve of the double yellow line to determine whether it had been reckless to drive. She decided she was fine. The swim and the purging had adequately cleared her head, and she sat further upright. She drove slower than usual, making sure not to lose sight of Sam's car ahead. Elsa was unsure where they were headed; she had not recognized the route for some time and wondered if she was drunk after all. Spotting red lights before her, she hit the brakes—sooner than necessary and harder than she'd meant—and followed Sam's car up a dirt drive which led to a small house surrounded by a large field. Elsa turned off the engine and sat in the dark. A gentle knock caused her to start. She turned to find Sam hovering beyond the glass and rolled down the window.

"Can I help you?" Elsa asked.

Sam smiled and rested their elbows on the open window.

"That was hot."

"What was?" Elsa asked, leaning her head against the headrest.

"Driving with you behind me."

Elsa laughed.

"Is this your house?"

"Not for much longer."

"Can I ask you a question?"

"Sure."

"Where's Sarah?"

Elsa had expected Sam to draw back at the inquiry, but they remained, their head filling the driver's-side window.

"She had to go back to the city. I'm closing up shop, so to speak."

"Hence the last-minute invite."

With a sincerity that surprised Elsa, Sam said, "I'm really glad you came." They leaned in and kissed her. "Any chance I can get you out of that car?"

Elsa laughed again. "Okay, watch out."

Sam righted, stepping aside to make room.

Inside was a small kitchen that opened up onto a living room. The large windows reflected back the room's lit interior. Original elements of the old house—an antique cream-colored stove, the wide beams of the floors and ceiling—contrasted with more modern conveniences, and Elsa had the sense that the home was curated specifically to be rented. Every corner of the house was correct and therefore lifeless, and Elsa felt damp and tired. Unsure where to sit, she decided on a stool facing the marble-topped island separating the kitchen from the living room and looked around for signs of Sarah, of what their life here had been like these past months, but the neatly clustered sofa and chairs, the abstract geometric artwork which hung on the walls, rebuked any closer reading. Sam rummaged inside the stainless steel fridge, emerging with two beers.

"It's all I've got," they said, waving the bottles back and forth, as if to tempt her. "Want some?"

"Sure."

Elsa didn't want the beer; she reached out to accept it. The kitchen's sleek appliances made her feel colder than she already was, and she wished to change into something dry. Though it would have been easy enough to ask, Elsa felt suddenly shy. Goose bumps formed on her arms, and she thought of the tidying expert.

Sam walked past her to sit on the sofa, and it took Elsa a moment to realize that she was meant to follow. She hesitated before sitting, feeling the backs of her pants.

"I'm still a little wet."

"It doesn't matter," Sam said with a wave of their hand, taking a sip of beer.

Elsa sat with her legs tucked underneath her, the damp fabric clinging to her thighs. She had no idea what hour it was, but it was late and her exhaustion was total.

"Whose house was that earlier tonight?"

"This guy named Roger," Sam said, leaning their head against the back of the couch. "The tall guy who was at the table with us on the porch toward the end. He's involved with the programming for the festival."

Elsa nodded. "And did you know everyone else there?"

She shifted her legs.

"Most," Sam replied. "If not by name then at least by sight. But basically everyone who stuck around was in or affiliated with Sarah's play. But I guess you knew that already," they continued after a moment.

The two looked at one another. Elsa lowered her gaze to her hand; without noticing, she had begun to peel the bottle's label, and bits of torn paper had accumulated there. She lifted her palm and blew the remnants into the air.

Sam let out a stunned laugh. They picked up a balled shred of paper which had landed in their lap and flicked it at Elsa, who batted it away. Their eyes met and Elsa smiled.

"Come here," Sam said, catching Elsa's wrist and pulling her in.

The two began to kiss, and Elsa felt Sam climb on top of her, her beer nearly spilling as they lifted a leg to straddle her. Elsa felt Sam tilt her chin upward, their lips finding Elsa's before gently kissing along her jawline. Sam kissed her mouth again and Elsa traced their lower back, their thighs, with her free hand.

Sam began to move their hips—only a hint at first, and then more boldly, and Elsa began to anticipate their movements. Sam pressed up against her stomach. Elsa was unsure where to put her hands, still holding her beer. Should she move her hips, or remain static, a stable object onto which Sam could perform their pleasure? Elsa placed a hand on their ass and began to kiss back, harder this time.

"I want you." Sam leaned back to look at Elsa.

"I want you too," she replied.

Their lips met, and Elsa felt Sam enter her mouth with their tongue, at first a suggestion and then more fully, as Elsa softened.

"Let's go to bed."

Sam rose and extended a hand. Elsa grabbed it and allowed herself to be hoisted from the sofa and led through the kitchen, into the small bedroom down the hall. Placing their beer on the nightstand, Sam did the same with Elsa's label-torn bottle, kissing her neck before pushing her onto the bed. Elsa laughed, letting her limbs grow limp.

Sam crawled on top of her before getting off the bed to unbutton Elsa's pants.

"Oh, shit," they said, tossing them to the floor. "These are wet."

Elsa lay on her back and stared up at the ceiling. Sam returned and knelt above Elsa, running a hand along the side of her face before shifting their weight on top of her. She closed her eyes and felt Sam's tongue on her lips, her clavicle, her nipple. She felt Sam reach down between her legs, realizing she was already wet, submitting to the pressure of their palm. Elsa felt Sam's mouth on her stomach, their forehead pressed into her. Kissing along the top of her pelvis, Sam's fingers touched the opening of her sex. Elsa felt them edge inside her and retreat slowly.

"Fuck."

Elsa pushed aside the embarrassment she felt at her utterance and opened her eyes. Sam stood to turn off the light and undressed before returning to sit beside Elsa on the bed. She dragged her hand gently down their spine.

"How do you want me to touch you?"

Without responding, Sam took Elsa's hand and guided it inside them. They were wet, open, more than the woman had ever been, or Elsa when she touched herself.

"More," they said. Elsa lifted herself to her knees and Sam lay their head back on the bed. She added a third finger.

The woman had always used a vibrator whenever she was alone with Elsa, a gently curved, palm-sized device, Elsa's fingers held steady inside. Elsa was uncertain now, her motions tentative.

Sam grabbed her wrist and began to fuck themself using her hand.

"Like this," they said. "Harder."

Elsa felt clumsy and hesitant but obeyed. She liked it slower, softer, a gentle building. Sam moaned, taking Elsa's free hand in their mouth. Elsa had been using it to prop herself up and momentarily lost her balance. Shifting her weight to her knees, her thighs tightened. She pictured the woman, knelt on the bed, back arched as the man stood behind her. Elsa had never learned to take it like the woman, who always wanted it harder, more.

Sam pulled Elsa's knuckles out of her mouth slowly.

"Elsa."

"What?"

"I mean it."

Their eyes found each other in the half-light of the room.

"Fuck me. I'm a big boy, I promise I can take it."

Elsa almost felt the words *I love you* slip out. She thought of the actor-character, using the full strength of her arm to perform Sam's pleasure. Her motions were strong and steady, a slight ache near her elbow. She was the man, the actor-character, Sam themself. She began to thrust, her elbow wedged at the crux of her hips; her hand was an extension of this thrusting. As her motions became more organic, forceful, Sam moaned and reached down to touch themself.

"I'm close. Don't stop."

Elsa said their name to herself: *Sam*. The name grew louder in her head, and she repeated it, her desire growing more acute. Elsa put her whole body into it. *Sam*, she said again to herself as she moved in and out of them, her hand a dildo, a tongue, a dick. Never before had she fucked the woman like this, never known herself capable.

Sam's name was in the air, and Elsa realized she had uttered it. She allowed herself to say it again, aloud. *Sam*: the name she had searched for over and over, like returning to a well. Memories flashed before her, like signposts which marked the passing of time. "Sam," she whispered, picturing trips to the coffee shop, their midnight swim, the touch of their hand on her knee. "Sam," she heard herself say, more loudly this time, as she reached for Sam's hair and pulled. The soft curve of Sam's back lifted off the mattress and their body shuddered. Elsa released them and they flopped back down on the bed.

"Holy shit," they said, propping themself on their elbows to look at her. They withdrew Elsa's fingers slowly, pressing them into their palm.

"Did you come?" she asked.

"You couldn't tell?"

They rose to their knees and pushed Elsa down on the bed beneath them.

"I wasn't sure you had it in you."

Sam slid two fingers inside her and Elsa reached for the headboard, pushing against it and rocking her hips, slowly at first and then harder, the bed creaking each time she pressed into it. She wove her free hand through Sam's hair once more.

"It drives me crazy when you say my name."

"Sam," Elsa said.

Each time her hips followed their steady motion, Elsa said their name, feeling the weight of Sam's body, the pressure of their mouth, the dampness from the swim which had mixed with their sweat and the fluids of their bodies. The coarse hairs of Sam's sex pressed themselves against her leg, Sam's fingers inside her.

"Sam," Elsa said, as she moved her hips.

Sam was wet against her.

"Sam," she said, again.

Their bodies, their excretions, were no longer their own but some third thing which they had conjured between them. Elsa was close, her hand guiding Sam's head, as she rocked back and forth beneath them. The clothes she had purchased flashed before her; she saw herself in them, walking with Sam down a city street. Elsa tried to focus once more on the sensations of their fucking. Sam was grinding against her, reaching further inside Elsa, Sam's spine visible in the dark, delineating the arch of their back.

Elsa was close; her hips moved underneath the mounting pressure.

"Sam," she said, though the name rang hollow. It had nothing to do with the person who was in bed with her. Sam let out a soft moan.

"I want you to come for me," they said, lifting their head before descending back into Elsa.

She felt their mouth on her, their lips on her inner thighs, their tongue between her legs, a steady force. Familiar images of Sam resurfaced, and this time Elsa allowed herself to follow their logic.

"Sam," she said, as she pictured their feed, the photos she had scrolled through on both phone and computer.

"Sam," she said, picturing them seated beside the actor-character, two dark figures on a rock.

"Sam," she said again, louder this time, her hips rocking, the sheets of the bed damp and twisted beneath their bodies. Sam began to moan harder as they pressed their weight into Elsa.

"Sam," Elsa said, almost a whisper, as she pictured Sam's dating profile, how she had swiped and waited, breathless. She thought of her favorite picture, the one in which Sam was looking to the side, smiling at a stranger beyond the frame.

Elsa imagined herself there—the receiver of this side glance, a secret passing between the two of them; her pleasure mounted. She clung to this image, moving her hips to meet Sam, their head cradled between her thighs.

"Sam," she called out. Elsa pictured the two of them, a shared look, and she came.

"Fuck," she said. "Fuck."

She lay back on the bed, arms and legs splayed out across the mattress. Her face and limbs had grown numb. Sam laid to rest their head on her stomach. Elsa followed their heartbeat against her thigh, running her hand through their hair as she turned to survey the clothes that cluttered the floor.

As Sam slept, Elsa looked around the darkened room. There had been a time when Elsa had slept easily in the beds of others; the reshuffling of varied interiors had formed a kind of backdrop to her days. She had found comfort in the itinerancy, as if doing research for a life to come. It was taken for granted that she would eventually arrive at the stage when she would be forced to purchase this sort of rug over another, one particular lamp, and thus make her mark. These decisions, she knew, would reveal something definitive about her, would make her legible to herself and others. Until then, she coasted through borrowed lives.

A vase of fresh flowers sat on top of a painted dresser by the far wall, next to a framed exhibition poster of an artist Elsa did not recognize. In spite of herself, she had grown accustomed to her childhood bedroom, and her current vantage point from Sam's bed unsettled her. Elsa thought of the months Sam had spent here with Sarah and turned toward their sleeping figure. Once Sam had fallen asleep, Elsa had retrieved her phone on the way to the bathroom; she reached for it now, easing onto her back and dimming the brightness in her settings. The light from the screen cast the rest of the room into total darkness, and the specificity of the space around her dissolved. She opened her social media and searched for Sam, turning to make sure they were still asleep.

Scrolling, she paused to enlarge the images she had grown to like the most. Even though Sam was now beside her, even though they had fucked, the sense of longing had not abated. Elsa moved her thumb to view their tagged images.

Sam turned over and Elsa drew the phone to her chest to cover the light. She waited. When she was certain that they were asleep, she lifted the device and typed in the handle for Sarah's profile. She scrolled in search of pictures of Sam. The uneasy feeling which crept up was not, she realized, guilt, but melancholy. She imagined Sarah and Sam, how they had met—at a party, Sam had told Elsa on their first date—and the fitful months of passion, of sleepless nights and giddy uncertainty that must have followed. Picturing it now, Elsa mourned this time on their behalf. She scrolled further, pausing on a picture of Sarah and Sam in the bright light of morning.

The couple appeared seated at a wooden picnic table, rain-worn and spotted with lichen. Elsa checked the date of the post—over three years ago. Sarah was seated to the left, nearly out of frame, Sam to the right; behind them was a grassy field that rose abruptly into rocky cliffs. The Alps, perhaps, or some other European mountain range, though Elsa couldn't be sure: there was no tagged location. The two straddled the bench, facing one another. The peaks jutted into the blue sky behind them. Sam was looking at Sarah, whose attention was directed elsewhere, her head tilted down—perhaps toward a book, or at some other object in her lap. They wore the peaceful expressions of morning, coffee mugs obscuring the bottom halves of their faces. A third cup hinted at the presence of another; the photographer.

Elsa zoomed in on the protrusion of Sam's ear, pale against the long, dark hairs tucked on either side. The sight of it made her weak.

Laying her phone down on her chest, she had the thought that she only knew how to approach love laterally, to find its prior existence and move in, rather than build it from the ground up. Her wish, it occurred to her now, was to experience love absent herself.

Elsa felt the urge to search online for the woman. It had been her who had initially brought up the possibility of Elsa joining their relationship, the topic broached over lunch downtown when it was just the two of them, a few days after the first night they had all slept together. It was proposed delicately—the woman was always so serious, everything done with much forethought. Elsa had never met someone who lived so entirely in her mind. It was only in bed or in sleep that Elsa remembered that the woman had a body, was maybe all body.

The woman laid out her proposal as a matter of fact: something had been lacking for a long time and they believed that Elsa was the missing piece. Meeting her, the woman said, had renewed the passion in their relationship: the two had been in a state of peaceful calm ever since their night with Elsa. They both felt, the woman continued, that heterosexual relationships made almost no sense, and neither did the inherent isolation of the nuclear family, or worse, the urban couple. So much more could be achieved by three than by two. The woman explained to Elsa that the very qualities that had attracted her to the man were also those she despised most, that she had been missing a feminine touch, the sort of understanding that only two women could share, something to temper the hard boundaries of their relationship.

Elsa, too, had felt all this: the alienating distance of masculinity, the acceptance of the limitations of ever being understood by a lover, and she said so, stopping as she did to find her words. As she spoke, the woman had reached for her hand underneath the table. Their fingers remained interlaced for the rest of the meal.

Elsa lay still, trying to match her breath to the rhythm of Sam's until dawn.

On her way home, scenes of their morning together replayed before Elsa—how she had remained awake until the sun filled the bedroom, wanting to inch closer to Sam's warm body, but not daring; how, when they woke, Sam had gotten out of bed straightaway and how Elsa felt thwarted, how she had wanted to reach out and touch them; how she had felt childish for wanting this, as she joined them in the kitchen instead, watching Sam move about as they prepared the coffee, which the two had drunk mostly in silence. To fill the space, Elsa had said she felt tired. Sam had said the same.

It was early when she left. Though she had nowhere else to be, when they had finished their coffees Elsa said that she'd better go to be polite. Sam had not deterred her, and so she found herself kissing them on the threshold, the morning grass still wet, a throbbing in her head, wishing to forestall the moment of her departure, to seek some kind of assurance—of affection or futurity, or at the very least a lack of regret—but she was unsure of how to ask for such things. Sam had said that they were leaving tomorrow, that they had enjoyed meeting Elsa, that she should keep in touch.

"You too," was all Elsa said in response. She had turned and made her way to her mother's car, finding it parked askew, the front tires crossing over the dirt and into the lawn.

Elsa drove according to Sam's directions until she found her bearings. Her phone had died at some point in the early morning. As she sped alongside the river that she had swum in the night before, she

253

could not help envisioning scenes with Sam which she knew would not occur. Though she had not slept, the coffee had made her alert and full of hope, and she felt the urge to drive somewhere, to punctuate the moment before heading home, but she could think of nowhere to go. She reached to play the pop music which had accompanied her drive to the mall, but remembered her phone was dead. Rolling down the windows, she let the warm air pass over her. At the memory of sex from the night before, Sam's fingers inside her, she felt her blood rush to her vulva: a warmth, a certain rawness, a slight ache which was not altogether unpleasant.

Elsa slammed the brakes. A fox had run into the road. Its fur was bright red in the morning sun and it stood, frozen and staring at Elsa, unsure of which way to run, turning back suddenly the way it had come and disappearing into the low bushes. As her pulse slowed, she began to drive. After the initial shock of animal and brakes, the encounter seemed to her a fortuitous omen.

When she entered the kitchen, Elsa was surprised to find both her parents standing around the island. Her father looked away; she met her mother's stare as she approached them. She held the borrowed keys out on her open palm, an offering, and her mother took them without speaking.

"It would have been nice to get a text," her father said after a moment.

"Sorry. My phone died."

"Where were you?" her mother asked.

Elsa leaned against the oven and looked over to Sasha, who entered the kitchen. She bent to pet her.

"I was at a party," she said, stroking the animal, and noted how Sasha's fur had grayed along the tip of her nose. "Sorry," she said again, looking up at both of her parents. "I ended up drinking and didn't think it was safe to drive."

"I was up half the night, you know—"

"Elaine—" her father cut in, a warning.

"What?" her mother asked.

Elsa found that she was ready for a fight, for her mother's composure to finally break. Her mother adjusted her stance and sighed.

"Your mother was worried, that's all," her father said, placing his hand on her mother's crossed forearm.

"Okay." Elsa stood.

"Next time, please send us a text." Her mother's voice had softened. "I had errands I was hoping to run this morning."

"I'm sorry," Elsa said.

"It's not so late. You can still run to the store before we have to head out, no?" her father asked.

"Where are you guys going?" Elsa looked from one to the other.

"It's fine," her mother sighed, reaching momentarily to stroke Elsa's hair before letting her hand drop between them.

Her mother grabbed her purse from the counter. Elsa and her father stood in silence until they heard the dull thud of the car door shutting, the faint start of the engine.

"Dad," Elsa said.

"Dad," she said again, when she received no response. Her father stared at the deserted entryway.

"Hm," he replied, turning to her.

"Where are you guys going?"

"We're playing tennis with the Andersons. And then over to theirs for lunch afterward."

"What day is it?" Elsa asked.

"Sunday."

"Oh," she said.

Her father reached out tentatively and squeezed her hand.

"Can I make you a coffee? It looks like you've had a long night."

"Yeah, sure. Okay."

He waved toward the stools tucked on the other side of the island to indicate that she should take a seat. She did.

"Thanks."

Elsa watched as he started the machine.

"Milk?" he asked, turning to face her.

"Yes, please."

She watched as he moved over to the refrigerator and back.

"One shot or two?" He held up a plastic pod.

"Two."

Her father grabbed a mug from the cabinet. Elsa watched as he pushed the lever.

"Did you have fun at least?"

His back was still turned to her.

"I can't tell," she said.

Her father laughed and placed the second pod in the machine. Elsa listened for the puncture and then the steady drip.

"That's true of most parties, I think," he said.

"I kind of met someone."

Her father turned toward the island and poured the milk into the mug.

"Do you want me to warm it up?" he asked.

"Sure," Elsa said.

"Am I allowed to ask who?"

"Just someone who was here for the festival." Her father moved over to the microwave. "But they're leaving. Or they've left. Or they'll leave tonight."

"That's too bad."

Her father pressed start and the two were silent for the duration. When the microwave signaled, he retrieved the mug and held it out to her.

"Thanks," Elsa said, taking it from him.

"But it's just one person this time?" her father asked, leaning against the counter, his arms crossed. "Call me old-fashioned, but that strikes me as simpler."

Elsa coughed, the espresso nearly spilling. "I didn't realize Mom had said anything."

Her father shrugged. "I'm too old to understand all that anyway."

They were silent. Elsa heard the tumble of ice being made in the freezer.

"I'm sorry this person is leaving, though. Either way," her father said.

Elsa could think of nothing else to say. She reached for her dead phone on the counter.

"I think I might go lie down if that's okay."

"Of course."

"Thanks for the coffee."

"Any time."

The will to leave overpowered her desire to remain, but only by a notch.

Elsa drove through town and past the restaurant. When she saw the turnoff to the swimming hole, she moved suddenly without signaling and heard the sharp pierce of a car horn from behind. Though there were no other cars, she drove slower now, past the farmhouse on the right whose grassy meadows descended at a steep slope to the dirt road. Through the open windows, she listened to the clinking of pebbles as they hit the bottom of her mother's car. She thought briefly of Sam, and of the man and the woman, and turned her attention instead to her hands on the steering wheel, the stark morning light illuminating the fine hairs on the backs of her knuckles. She tried to take in its warmth.

When she arrived, an SUV was parked on the grass. Elsa turned off the engine and heard voices rising from the water below. Closing her eyes, she became attuned once more to the faint pulsing in her sex. A flash of memory: Sam astride her. She heard the happy cry of a child followed by a large splash; a mother's voice called back in response. Elsa sat for a few minutes, listening to the rise and fall of their voices and the sound of bodies moving through water, before she turned the engine on and began to drive away. She decided she would take the long way home, along the dirt road, past the stretch of fields on either side. The morning sunlight dappled the way before her. Ascending the hill, she slowed to pass an older couple heading the opposite direction, holding hands. A large dog trotted off leash in front of them. They waved and she returned the gesture. Hers was the only car on the road.

ACKNOWLEDGMENTS

To the tidying experts and vloggers not mentioned by name in this book, thank you to Marie Kondo, Devon Lee Carlson, and Emma Chamberlain. Thanks to the unnamed film, *Call Me by Your Name*, and its leading actor-character, Timothée Chalamet. You were my first gay crush, a gateway drug for so many. Lastly, thank you to Lauren Berlant's *Cruel Optimism* for providing me with a framework and a language for so much of what I was grasping at in the nascent stages of this novel.

Thank you to Anna Hogeland and Shelby Kinney-Lang for their early and continued support throughout the process of writing this book. I doubt whether I would have had the stamina or assurance to finish without your encouragement or example.

For pointing out all of my worst linguistic tics and syntactical crutches, thanks are owed to David Richardson; there wasn't a page left unmarked, and the work is so much better for it. (Also, thank you for telling Anna Stein she really should get around to reading it.)

To my parents, Amy and Chris, thank you for housing me while I fumbled my way through my first book, and for showing me what a life dedicated to reading and writing could look like. Thank you to Hailey Newbound for putting a fire under me; you are a continual source of inspiration.

For taking a chance on a manuscript that still needed work, and for shepherding this project through, I am especially indebted to my agents, Anna Stein and Julie Flanagan. To my editors, Olivia Taylor-Smith and Allegra LeFanu, thank you for your editorial insights, your patience, and your unwavering faith. Additional thanks to Brittany Adames and the rest of the team at Simon & Schuster.

Finally, thank you to Milo Wippermann for their steady confidence, their brilliance, and their bravery in writing and in life; so much of what is good in this book is the result of your effort and care. For the countless hours of line edits, the hand holding, and for pushing me and the manuscript always further, I am forever indebted to you.

About the Author

MADISON NEWBOUND is a writer and server living in Brooklyn. *Misrecognition* is her first novel.